SUM....

RIVKA SPICER

For further works by this author, please see the bibliography at the end of this book.

Prologue

March Week 2
By Elise Waterford

A couple of days ago a rapper asked me to write him a haiku. Well, he put it on Twitter and I took up the challenge. I was on my own, I was bored...you get the picture. It was both challenging and, surprisingly, fun. Haiku is probably the most pointlessly addictive pastime after Sudoku. Those Japanese sure know how to reel people into procrastination!

So after sending my little ditty off to said rapper I found myself jotting down more lines. The first one I came out with was this:

> *Bleak and hollow I*
> *Desolate in loneliness*
> *Thus my heart...silence*

I mean that right there is some depressing stuff, right? I read it back and, while I thought that poetically it was beautiful, I think I really need to get a grip on myself; bend the laws of physics to boot myself up the ass. I'm too old for all the emo stuff. If I'm feeling that low then I should do something about it.

So I figured I'm just lonely. I'm a woman. I've got needs and a biological clock that's ticking so damn loudly I can barely hear myself think. I'm hardly going to meet the man of my dreams in this backwater town in the frozen tundras of the north, so the next logical thing is to sign up to a dating site. After all, it's worked for so many people I know!

I get myself online and look up a site I know caters to the north of Scotland. I flick through the first page and by the end of it I'm feeling a thousand times better about myself. Not because I think this is the answer, but because if that is the standard of singles out there then there's hope for me yet to find a man before I have to go online! I'm not unattractive – I'm slim and my hair is a nice glossy shade of brown. I guess my eyes are quite nice too. At first I thought I was being unfair but on a second (and then third) reading they were still as awful as I thought they were and those were the ones that weren't so illiterate I could barely make out what they were saying.

A few examples...

Hi, my name is .... and I'm one of those nice guys you're always reading about.... (Excuse me while I go throw up.)

Hi, my name is .... I'm a caring guy and I don't like football. (Seriously?? That's the second thing you say to a prospective partner???)

But my personal favourite:

Hi, my name is .... and I have a son but he doesn't live with me.

Really? Really??? Totally aside from the fact that most women would read that and think 'oh great, you knocked some woman up and then left her. Classy guy...classy', I don't know what's worse – the fact that this is the one defining feature about him or the fact that he actually wrote that this was the one defining feature about him.

My disbelief gave way to amusement and then to a weird maternal instinct to want to gather these men up and explain to them how to do it properly. I'm sure there must be a call for coaching in this department. Kind of like Hitch at an early intervention stage. I could be that woman. How hard can it be? We all know the obvious – if a woman describes herself as bubbly you know she's chubby. It's par for the course.

So I thought I'd practice what I'd say if I was writing a blurb about me. What is my defining feature? Straight off I'd have to say it's my creativity. I guess I'd start with something along the lines of "Hi, my name is Elise. I'd like to think I'm a weaver of words and when I'm not at my day job you can find me doing one of my many hobbies. I am a columnist and a novelist. I love to dance, play my guitar and I'm also a good cook."

See, right there are several different topics of conversation to broach. They make me an interesting person I think. Those four sentences tell you what's most important to me at the same time as letting on that I lead a full and slightly off the wall life. I also hope the fact that everything has the correct spelling and (mostly correct) grammar will deter anyone intimidated by an articulate woman.

Of course, I might come across as a total nerd who has nothing better to do than sit home alone writing stuff, but that's a risk I'll take if it has the benefit of finding me someone with similar interests.

There's always then the risk of finishing the blurb with something that will scare prospective partners away. I could have the best opening in the world and still not get a single bite from the fishpond of life if I finished it with "I'm desperate to get married and have 7 babies" or "I don't want you in my life but since you come attached to your tool and I want some of that, it's not like I get a choice...".

Of course I would NEVER say such things. I am a lady after all...It's one of those occasions when simple, classic elegance wins the day. I'm looking for fun that might blossom into something more.

Chapter 1

The phone rang and Elise jerked awake suddenly. Blearily she checked the number but it wasn't in her contacts, so she silenced it and chucked it back on the bedside table, ready to return to sleep. Honestly, who called at this time of the morning? People shouldn't be allowed to use any form of communication before at least 8am.

Five minutes later it rang again, the same number. Annoyed, Elise silenced it again and tried to go back to the dream she had been having before being so rudely interrupted. It wasn't until the third time it rang that she finally wondered if it was some sort of emergency. Perhaps one of her parents was sick or her friend Fern needed help.

"Hello?" She mumbled sleepily, not even lifting her head from the pillow.

"Ms Waterford?" The woman at the other end sounded ridiculously perky, clearly a product of expensive caffeine, and Elise sighed.

"Yeah. Speaking."

"Ms Waterford, my name is Nikki. I'm calling from the offices of Monochrome Magazine."

"Seriously?" Elise squinted at the clock with one eye. "You're at work at twenty past six in the morning? Girl, I hope they pay you well."

There was an awkward silence as though Nikki wasn't sure whether to be confused or amused and then she continued in the same singsong voice. "Ms Waterford, am I right in thinking you are currently at home in Scotland?"

"Yeah, I'm at home. Why? Where else would I be at this ungodly hour of the morning?" Uhuh, because *that* didn't make her sound like someone sworn to celibacy...This conversation was getting weirder by the second.

"Excellent. One of our editors is visiting Scotland at the moment and he spotted your column in the local courier. He was impressed with your writing style and would like to arrange a meeting to discuss a proposal with you."

"A proposal?" It was too early to talk business, surely? Elise finally sat up, trying to clear her thoughts a little. "What sort of proposal?"

"Business." Nikki left out the 'obviously' but it was hinted at. "We understand you are a freelance writer. He has some work he would like to discuss with you."

The enormity of the conversation was starting to sink in. "For Monochrome?" It was the magazine with the largest circulation in Europe. Part fashion, part gossip, part gritty and hard hitting journalism, it was a little of something for everyone. Getting a job as a writer for Monochrome was the Holy Grail for journalists and columnists alike.

"In part. It's really up to Mr Stone to explain the details to you. I'm his secretary. When would you be free to meet with him?"

"Where is he?" Most English people have no idea how big Scotland is so Elise was pleasantly surprised when Nikki said this Mr Stone was skiing in Aviemore. That was only just over two hours away. "I've got stuff planned for today but I can get there around lunchtime tomorrow."

"Excellent." Elise could hear the clacking of a keyboard in the background. "I'll organise a room for you at the chalet. He said to pass on that the snow is still quite deep and current temperatures are below freezing so he advises you to pack warmly."

"Pack?" It was fast becoming the most surreal conversation Elise had ever had. "How long is this interview? I thought I was just going for a couple of hours."

"He needs to spend some time with you to decide if the idea will work," she explained as though that was adequate. "It won't be more than three days as he's due back here for a meeting on Monday."

"Right." Elise didn't know what else to say. "I guess I'll pack a bag then."

She passed on her email address for Nikki to send her directions and details and then hung up, staring at the phone in her hand in disbelief. Short of a rainfall of spatulas, the day just couldn't get any weirder.

Elise arrived in Aviemore just after midday the following day and followed the directions she had printed out through the pretty little village and into the chalets. When she thought she'd arrived, she peered out of the window and decided there must have been some mistake. The building was gorgeous. The ground floor was stone built with a wrap-around porch on 2 sides and upstairs there was a balcony all around the outside of an oak upper floor with huge windows that spilled out golden light onto the drifting snow. It was huge and it looked like it belonged on a Christmas card. It had to be the wrong place.

She looked at the directions again, wondering where she had gone wrong, and then someone tapped on her window. It was so unexpected she startled and bashed her wrist on the steering wheel.

She cursed loudly. "Ow!" Cradling it ruefully she looked out the window at a guy who might as well have just stepped off the skiing edition of GQ magazine. He was ruggedly handsome and she didn't need to see a price tag to know his clothes cost more than what she earned in a year. From his artfully tousled blond hair to his striking blue eyes, he was every inch the kind of guy that would stay in a chalet like this. And she had just sworn at him. Loudly. Damn it. "I'm sorry." She blurted out, rolling down the window. "I'm lost and I was looking at the directions and I didn't see you sneaking up on me. Not that you sneaked up on me. I just didn't see you. Sorry." She snapped her mouth shut before she said anything else idiotic. He just grinned at her, revealing unsurprisingly perfect white teeth. Elise silently vowed never to open her mouth again.

"Where were you aiming for?" His voice wasn't particularly deep but it was melodious. Mutely, Elise handed over her print-out and he scanned it quickly before breaking out in a chuckle. "No, you're definitely in the right place, Ms Waterford. I'm Taylor Stone."

"Oh." Elise blinked and inwardly cursed again for swearing in front of him. "Wow, sorry. Nice to meet you." Awkwardly she stuck her hand out the window to shake his and he laughed.

"You too. Did you bring much luggage?"

"Uh, no." He backed up so she could open the door and she climbed out. "Just one bag and my guitar."

"You brought your guitar? Excellent!" He seemed genuinely pleased but Elise still felt about an inch tall. If she'd known he was going to be this handsome she would have totally packed different clothes and left her guitar at home, but now that it was here she couldn't leave it in the car because the cold would damage it. As though sensing her discomfort, he smiled again. "When I read in your column that you played, I had hoped you would bring it. Mine is in my room – it's been a while since I had anyone to jam with."

Despite herself Elise was astonished. "You play too?"

"I know." He shrugged good-naturedly as he hauled her overnight bag out of the boot. "I don't look the type to play the guitar but I learned at school when it was the cool thing to do and now it's what I do to relax. Come on in."

He waited for her to pull her guitar case out and then led her up the steps and into the house. Warmth enveloped them like a blanket and once they had put her things by the stairs he took her coat and hung it by the door.

"May I call you Elise?" He asked and she nodded.

"Of course."

"Excellent. And you must call me Taylor, none of this Mr Stone nonsense. Makes me feel like my dad. Are you hungry? I'm assuming you haven't had lunch?"

"No I haven't eaten. It was only 10 when I left."

"Excellent. Well the girls have laid something out for us to eat so I'll put the kettle on and take you on a tour of the house."

"The girls?" Elise asked, following him through to the kitchen. "Are there other people staying?"

He looked at her, amused. "No, I meant the chalet girls. There are two of them. They keep the place clean and feed me on a regular basis so I don't waste away in between all my skiing."

"Oh. That's good. Perfect holiday then." Elise smiled, feeling like she'd landed on another planet but her host seemed so nice and he chuckled gently.

"Yeah, it's pretty relaxing not having to do anything except enjoy myself."

"And conduct job interviews..." She reminded him and he shrugged.

"That could be enjoyable." He grinned. "It's less a job interview and more a question of my getting your measure as a person but we'll talk about that over lunch." He flicked the switch on the kettle and then took her on a tour of the chalet. It looked huge on the outside but there weren't that many rooms, although the rooms in themselves were all large. Elise's bedroom was about six times the size of her room at home, if you counted the dressing area and en-suite bathroom with a tub big enough for a rugby team. Everything was beautifully but expensively furnished in warm cream and biscuit tones and Elise tried not to gape too much at the luxuries.

By the time they returned to the kitchen the kettle was boiled and Taylor made up a cafetiere of coffee while Elise gazed out of the window.

"Have you been here before?" Taylor asked and Elise shook her head.

"No. I've never been skiing. I've driven past plenty of times on the way down south to visit family but I've never actually stopped at Aviemore. It's pretty isn't it?"

"Yes it is." He fitted the lid to the cafetiere. "I try and come up here at least once every winter, twice if I can get the time off. We'll go skiing tomorrow. So why Scotland? Your accent says you're not from these parts and your family live down south. Why did you move to the middle of nowhere?"

"I just fancied a change." Elise shrugged. "I was young and on my own. I had a little money from publishing my first book so I thought I'd use it to buy my first home and this was the only area I could afford to buy. It seemed like a great adventure at the time."

"And now?"

"Now?" She shrugged. "Moving up here was the best thing I ever did. I love it. I love my home and my friends and I love the peace and quiet but lately I've really been missing civilisation. I miss being twenty minutes from a cinema and being able to go to evening classes. I miss proper clubs and going to the theatre. It's quite easy up here to get sucked into being a hermit." She helped him carry the food through to a small dining area with a window that looked out across the hills.

"I have all those things living in London but I find it too much to take all the time. That's why I come away up here or other quiet places when I can." Taylor admitted easily, handing her a plate. "Tuck in."

"I guess it's hard to strike a happy balance." Elise mused, piling her plate with food. "There are so few places where you can get the illusion of peace and quiet whilst still being within minimal commuting distance of a large city. And when you do find places like that they're expensive to live in. Too expensive for people like me anyway."

"Maybe one day you'll be able to afford a house in the West Country." He grinned. "Sooner rather than later if what I have in mind works out."

"And what is it you have in mind?" Elise put down the sandwich she was eating. "I must say, I was surprised to get a call from your magazine. It was totally unexpected. I've never taken my writing seriously enough to make a submission to your offices."

"It was one of those little moments of serendipity." His tone was light but serious. "I came away to think about the direction of certain aspects of the magazine and happened to read your little article in the local paper about internet dating. It made me laugh so I called the office and had them email me all your recent columns. It's your style that I'm interested in as much as the content. It's the way you speak to the reader as though they're right there having a conversation with you. Monochrome is going from strength to strength. Our circulation numbers continue to increase and we're expanding overseas too, but for some reason the website isn't doing so well. We've done a load of market research yaddah yaddah blah blah blah" he waved dismissive hands "and discovered that people seem to respond better to sites with real people on them. They don't want faceless articles...that's what they buy the magazines for. They want to read about people's lives."

"We're talking about blogs, right?" She tried not to moan with delight as her tastebuds got a load of the most amazing sandwich she'd ever eaten.

"Exactly." His eyes twinkled when he smiled. "I'd been considering how to go about attaching blogs to the site. We can't just ask people to guest blog – there needs to be some sort of accompanying feature in the magazine. That's where you come in. This summer we're going to be running a series of features under the umbrella theme of 'summer loving'. I'd like one of those features to be your idea about coaching guys who are totally inept at internet dating. 6 weeks, 6 guys, thrice weekly blogs, 2 page spreads in the magazines. Once the 6 weeks are up we'll go back to see how they're doing, one by one, maybe track the dates that we hope they'll get. Overall it will be a 12 week contract across 3 editions of the magazine."

"That sounds awesome." She was delighted – it was a great idea for a feature. "So who are you going to get to do the coaching?"

He burst out laughing. "Well you of course! That's the whole point. I want you to help these guys and blog about it as you're going along."

Elise's jaw dropped. "Me? But...I'm single! I'm not exactly a successful advert for internet dating am I?"

"That's not the point." He settled back in his chair. "Going by what you wrote in your column it seems that most of these guys have forgotten they're trying to attract a woman and are just putting about themselves the first thing that comes into their head. Who better to tell them what to write than a single woman looking for a man, who can see and correct the mistakes they've made?"

"I just..." Elise didn't know what to say. "I guess I'm having a hard time seeing myself as a dating guru. I've been on my own for almost 3 years."

"Well we'll see how it goes these next few days." His tone said he thought she was worrying over nothing. "If I think we can work with you then that's exactly what we'll do – work with you. You'll be getting a lot of support and you'll have to do very little for the actual articles. It's mostly the blog you'll be working on. Of course you'll have to come to London for the 3 months. How would you feel about that? It will be paid for in expenses obviously so you don't need to worry about it."

"I don't mind coming to London for 3 months." Elise's heart was actually singing at the prospect of theatres and decent restaurants for a whole 3 months but she had to keep it grounded. She had 3 days in which to royally mess this up yet and, bearing in mind that the first word she had said to her potential new boss was the F word, it wasn't looking good.

As though reading her mind he reached across the table. "How is your wrist?" He took it gently and angled it into the sunlight, turning it slowly so he could check it over. "It looks a little bruised. You hit it pretty hard."

"It aches a little but I'm sure it'll be fine." She smiled reassuringly but he frowned.

"Maybe we should take you down to the doctors, get it checked over."

"No really, it'll be fine. It doesn't hurt much at all." She protested. He looked her straight in the eye.

"I would be happier if we got it looked at." He said with finality. "It's already bruised. You might have fractured it. If you're going to play your guitar and go skiing with me tomorrow I want to know that it's okay." Elise sighed. It was going to be a long 3 days.

Luckily the doctor saw them pretty quickly after lunch and examined Elise's wrist. "It's hard to say." He told them both. "Going by the bruising I suspect there is a fracture but, if there is, it's a hairline rather than a clean break. You'd better get it X-rayed just to be on the safe side."

So off they went to the hospital 16 miles away in Grantown on Spey. Taylor looked so serious as they waited to go in that Elise couldn't help but poke fun at him. "This has got to be the worst job interview EVER." She grumbled, trying not to laugh. "First I swear at you and then I maybe break my wrist and accuse you of sneaking up on me. We get to spend an afternoon in the hospital and if it is broken I have totally put a crimp in your ambitions to be a ski instructor. Could I have flunked it in any more epic style?"

"You haven't had a wardrobe malfunction yet." He kept a straight face for all of 5 seconds before creasing with laughter and bumping shoulders good-naturedly with her. "Well, it's not a conventional job interview, that's for sure. Perhaps we should just forget about the guys and just do a blog feature about you entitled tales of the unexpected..."

Unfortunately the X-ray showed a small crack in the wrist bone. It was too small to warrant putting in a cast but they did strap it up to prevent any more swelling and warned her to take it easy for the next few weeks.

"So, no skiing for you this time." Taylor sighed as he started up his car. "It'll have to be next winter now."

"Do you take all your employees skiing?" Elise asked before she could stop herself and Taylor grinned.

"No but then I don't normally conduct 3 day interviews in the middle of my holidays either. These are exceptional circumstances. If I didn't enjoy your column so much I wouldn't be taking such a big risk on you and, having read your column, I feel like I know a fair bit about you. I guess I'm predisposed to think of you as a friend because that is how you address your readers."

"Well I guess I won't be an employee any more next winter so it won't matter." Elise pointed out and Taylor looked sideways at her.

"You may well be an employee next winter if the blog is successful. There's nothing to say we won't extend your contract and you can blog from anywhere in between features."

"We'll see." Elise refused flatly to be thrilled at the prospect. "A lot of things could happen between now and then."

"True." He flashed her a quick grin as they left the car park. "You have another two hundred and something bones you could possibly break."

She had to laugh.

They spent the afternoon drinking coffee and discussing writing projects, music and places they had been. Turns out they didn't have much in common at all. They came from totally different backgrounds. The Stones were wealthy business magnates whereas Elise's family were just regular middle class working people. He had gone to the best schools and travelled to exotic places all over the world whereas Elise had stayed mostly in Europe. He had ruthlessly worked his way up to the position of editor whereas Elise had just gone alone and done her own thing quietly. They couldn't have been more different and yet they seemed to get along famously.

"You're not like anyone I've met before." Taylor announced expansively after his fifth glass of wine that evening. They were sat on the balcony under a patio heater watching the snow falling in the darkness over the hills while he gently strummed his guitar. "Most people in this business aren't very honest but you? You're so blunt it's almost painful."

"That's why you're the editor of the UK's most successful magazine and I'm a nobody writer for a tiny independent paper in the frozen north." Elise joked half-seriously. "I have ambitions but I'm not ruthless and if I'm really honest they don't involve anyone else."

"What do you mean?"

"Well..." she struggled to find the words. "I never wanted to work for a corporation. When I was 14 I wrote my first book. It was awful but the feeling I got when I'd finished it? Like nothing else on earth...I was hooked. From then on all I have ever wanted was to be an author but I hit the same problems as everyone else. It's so hard. You really have to be exceptional and back then I wasn't. I got one book published but after a brief spell on the bestseller lists it vanished into total obscurity. I started writing columns and articles to pay the bills when I left University and, as much as I enjoy it, part of me still dreams of being a novelist. I stayed a freelancer, even when I was offered jobs by papers. You, on the other hand, have always worked for the corporation. From my perspective, which could be totally wrong, you've made a career of it, from magazine to magazine. Being an editor is a career choice, not a vocation. You are the company, I am the lone writer."

"You're wrong." He blinked. "Actually you're right about most of it, but being an editor is more of a vocation than a career choice. To do it and do it well you really have to be passionate about what you do and how you influence people. It's a position of immense power, especially at a magazine as influential as Monochrome. Having to anticipate what the public wants when the public itself doesn't know what it wants is 1 part common sense to 2 parts guesswork and 5 parts alchemy."

"Alchemy huh?" Elise laughed. "I never thought of it as being mysterious or magical but I guess you're right. It's as much about you telling the public what they want as the public deciding for themselves. I've seen The Devil Wears Prada. I know how a particular shade of blue can filter down into the collective psyche. Should I pity your assistants?" She suddenly remembered Nikki of the perky voice who had been at work at 6am.

He smiled easily. "Well, I'm not that demanding or unnecessary at work but I guess I can be kind of scary as the submission deadline approaches."

"Your secretary was in work at 6am and you don't think that's demanding?" Elise burst out laughing. "What time do you let her go home? 2am?"

"I have a secretary on around the clock in the week before the deadline." He explained, not taking any offence. "She was probably coming off the night shift. That week is usually a crazy rush so I have 4 secretaries on rotation to keep track of everything."

"Do you make them fetch you coffee?" She couldn't help but poke fun and he sighed mockingly.

"No, I have an incredibly expensive coffee machine in my office. I make my own. Unless one of them wants coffee and they make one for me while they're at it."

"Good to know."

He strummed a few more bars on his guitar. "It's a shame you hurt your wrist. I would have liked to hear you play."

"I'll have my guitar in London if I get the job." Elise sipped her wine and settled back in her chair. "I never go anywhere without it. If I don't get the job then you'll have to wait until next winter and if we're still friends by then I'll come down and visit you when you come up to ski."

"There were a lot of 'if's in that." He plucked a blues riff. "I appreciate the job is a massive decision to make on both our parts but why do you think we wouldn't be friends by next winter? We've had a good day, haven't we?"

"Apart from the bit where I swore at you and broke my wrist?" She couldn't help the cheeky smile that crept out. "Yeah, I'd say that was a good day..."

He burst out laughing. "I guess that's true...your body might not withstand a friendship where you break stuff constantly. We shall have to hope it's a one time thing."

"That or I'll wear a bubble wrap suit every time I come near you." Elise joked and they both chuckled over the image for a while. "Anyway, I hope you'll still go skiing without me tomorrow." She continued when they had amused themselves into silence. "I have a couple of things to write so I can get on with that. You've come all the way up here so it would be a crying shame to spend your skiing trip stuck indoors."

"Okay. There are loads of books in my room too so if you get bored feel free to choose something to read. I'll prop the door open for you."

"Thanks."

"And there's plenty of food in the kitchen if you get hungry. I'll be back for lunch."

"Okay."

"And I'll leave a number on the kitchen table in case you need anything."

"Taylor I'll be fine. Stop fussing!" She laughed and he actually blushed.

"I've never been accused of fussing before." He admitted and she smiled at him.

"It's very charming, but really...I'll be fine. I'm going to head to bed now. See you tomorrow."

He got to his feet like a good gentleman. "Sleep well."

"You too."

Chapter 2

The following morning when Elise dragged herself out of bed at 9am Taylor was already on the slopes. She ate the breakfast that had been left out for her and settled in front of a window with her laptop to work on her column. Her wrist was painfully stiff and she gently massaged it in between sentences. It took almost three times as long as usual to write up and by the time Taylor got back at lunch time she was ready for a break.

"You're not looking so happy." He greeted her cheerfully, shedding clothes as he stepped through the door. "How's the wrist?"

"Stiff and a little sore." She admitted, helping him gather his snow gear up. "Typing was tough."

"That's a shame. I was hoping to set you a challenge this afternoon while I'm out."

"I could type it one handed." She protested. "What's the challenge?"

He grinned broadly at her. "I want you to write my profile. As in a profile for a dating site."

"Okay...maybe my wrist isn't that great..." Elise joked and he started to laugh.

"Come on...I need to know if you're perceptive enough to make this work. You're going to have one week with each guy for the feature and you're not going to be with them for all that time. I'm curious to see what your impressions are."

"I'll try but don't expect any great shakes. I haven't been quizzing you like I would one of my projects." She hung his jacket up on the pegs in the hall and followed him through to the kitchen. "Don't you think this might be a little awkward?"

"In what way?" He flicked the kettle on and started spooning coffee into a press.

"Well we might end up working together. Do you really want me to try and write about what I think women would find attractive about you?"

"Ahhh" He lifted an eyebrow. "You're concerned that I might think *you* find those things attractive about me?"

"Maybe." She was blushing and pretended to look out the window to cover it.

"Don't worry. This is strictly professional. I know you mean it objectively. We're both adult enough to know that mixing business with pleasure is totally out of bounds."

Elise winced inwardly. It was like being in a candy store with no money watching this gorgeous and rich guy parading around in front of her and being definitively told there was no hope of romance. Ever. It was almost depressing.

"Okay, I'll try. But like I said, don't expect anything great."

My name is Taylor and I live in London. I'm a successful executive but in my free time I like to be active. I have a lot of interests and like to keep up with current affairs but I also have a quirky side. I'm into fashion and I make excellent coffee. I love living in the city and eat out often, but I like to get away for quiet time in the country when work allows. Underneath my executive exterior lurks something of a free spirit. In the summer I like to go surfing and play my guitar on the beach while the sun goes down. There's something pretty special about watching the moon rise to the sound of the ocean. In the winter I like to ski and head up to Scotland whenever I can for some fun on the slopes. I'm intelligent and demanding, but I like to think that it's tempered with unfailing generosity. I volunteer when I can and am active in fundraising circles. I don't know how to cook, but I appreciate good food and really good wine.

I'm looking for a woman who can fit into both my worlds, someone with the panache, style and polish to glow in city life, but with enough creativity and laissez-faire to amuse herself and be content with the quiet times too. I want someone who will challenge me when I'm getting too big for my boots but will, at the same time, understand that my work plays a big role in my life and sometimes I have to work long hours. I like to date the old-fashioned way – coffee, dinner, a trip to the theatre...and I'm big on opening doors. There's a lot to be said for good manners. I'd also like to have children some day. If you'd like to get to know me...blah blah blah

When Taylor returned from the slopes Elise was in the kitchen with the two chalet girls, Sam and Susie, helping to cook dinner, so he left them to it and went for a shower. When he re-emerged the table was set and Elise was standing at the window absent-mindedly flexing her wrist.

"Aren't you supposed to be resting that?" he asked gently and she jumped, so lost in her thoughts she hadn't heard him come in.

"Yeah I am. It just aches. Sorry."

He grinned. "Don't apologise. I wasn't telling you off yet."

Humour quirked her lips. "Yet being the operative word there. Before long you'll be snapping at me every time I twitch my fingers."

He pretended to be offended. "Do you really think I'm that much of a control freak?"

"Well I couldn't put it in your dating profile because it would scare people away, but yes...I think you have to be for your job."

"Oh yes, the profile." He gestured for her to take a seat at the table as Sam came in to serve up the dinner. "How did you get on with it?"

"I don't know," she replied honestly. "I think I made some educated guesses that could be totally off the mark. If it's all correct, I should go into a career as a psychic."

"I was going to wait until after dinner, but now I'm intrigued." He put down his soup spoon. "Where is it? Can I read it now?"

Suddenly shy, Elise shrugged. "The laptop is in the living room. I left it up on the screen."

He went to fetch it and sat back at the table to read it while Elise ate her soup and tried not to watch him too obviously. For a really long time he just stared at the screen and Elise started to worry. It was only a couple of paragraphs...surely it hadn't taken him that long to read it?

"Did I get it right?" she ventured eventually when he didn't seem inclined to speak and he blinked at her.

"I don't even...how...?" He seemed at a loss for words.

"Damn, I got it all wrong didn't I?" Elise sighed. "I'm sorry. I'll try again tomorrow."

"No it's not that at all." He seemed a little dazed. "Totally the opposite in fact. How did you know this stuff? We've never talked about surfing. It's so weird, all the hairs are standing up on the back of my neck."

"The surfing was an educated guess." Elise tried to downplay it for fear of freaking him out. "It's all about observation. When you came home for lunch today you were wearing a T-shirt with a Fat Face logo on it. There's a pair of flip-flops peeking out from under your bed, which I noticed on the tour of the chalet yesterday. And when we were outside last night, you were playing Tom Petty. A lot of people who are into skiing are also into surfing."

"And the volunteering?"

"Okay, I confess that wasn't even an educated guess." She blushed. "You just seem like a generous kind of guy. Not everyone would put a total stranger up in such luxurious surroundings for three days and you seemed to know your way around the hospital pretty well yesterday."

"Ok." He blinked. "I know I told you I couldn't cook but how did you know I'm into wine?"

"There are two empty bottles of vintage Chateau Musar and an empty bottle of Chateau Margeaux waiting to go to the recycling. They'd only be chosen by somebody that knows more about wine than how much it costs. If you were going by price alone there'd be more expensive bottles sitting there."

"How do you know I'm looking for someone that will challenge me?" He had totally forgotten his soup by now and was staring at her as though she was the oracle.

"Because you laugh at me every time I answer back. I imagine you get a little fed up of everyone kow-towing to you all day every day at the office. It's not too much of a stretch of the imagination to think you'd want a woman that would keep you grounded when your world is threatening to turn you into a megalomaniac."

"The old-fashioned dating?" He shook his head. "I'm pretty sure I've never opened a door for you."

"True, but you did stand up when I left for bed last night. That speaks of ingrained gentlemanly manners. If that's what you do when you're not trying to impress someone, I suspect that you on a full-scale charm offensive would be terribly proper. I bet you expect girls to wait for you to come around and open their car doors for them too."

"Is that a bad thing?" He didn't mean it to sound snappy and she didn't take it as such.

"Not at all. On the contrary, it's very charming."

He grinned. "Right answer. Who says I'm not trying to impress you? And the kids? I know for a fact we haven't talked about that."

"Also a total guess on my part." She shrugged self-consciously. "I think guys from wealthy families are almost expected to pass the name on. In your case it's doubly important because you're an empire builder and that attitude nearly always extrapolates to daily life. Guys who have made something of their life want someone to pass it on to."

He stared at her in silence for a long time again. Feeling uncomfortable for reasons she couldn't fathom, Elise returned to her soup and tried to ignore his scrutiny. He waited until she had finished and their bowls were cleared away before he spoke again.

"You are one very scary woman. You're also hired."

They spent the evening watching a movie and both went to bed early. The following morning Elise's wrist was still stiff and aching so she spent most of the morning soaking in the swimming pool masquerading as a bath, pampering herself. By the time Taylor got back for lunch she was settled on a sofa in the living room reading.

"You're looking much happier today." He commented. "Is the wrist better?"

"Not really. I just haven't done any typing today." She smiled at him. "I figured it would help in case you decided to give me another challenge for the afternoon. You know I'm perceptive but you don't know if I can write a blog."

"Sure I do." He went straight for the coffee. "You write your columns like most people would write a blog. You just have to submit three a week instead of one. You think you could manage that?"

"I don't know." Elise frowned. That would certainly be hard work in between visiting her projects. "It'll be different when I have the theme given to me. Usually it takes me a couple of days a week to find something I want to write about. I also don't know how much editing it's going to need."

He poured her a coffee and placed it on the table in front of her. "Fine. I have every faith that you'll be excellent at it but if you want a challenge then I'd like you to write a blog entry about coming here. I'll read it when I get in this afternoon."

I have always thought that I'm not very photogenic. It grieves me when I see pictures of my friends looking all glossy and glamorous. It's a sharp kind of envy, like the way it feels to be the ugly teenager standing by the wall watching everybody else on the dance floor. It wasn't until the day before yesterday that I finally understood why I'm not photogenic. No, it's not a result of bad genes or frizzy hair and terrible clothing choices. It's because my life is such a disaster when you break it down into its constituent snapshots.

The day before yesterday I arrived for an interview. Literally within twenty seconds of meeting my prospective employer I had sworn at him, accused him of sneaking up on me, broken my wrist and made myself out to be directionally challenged. As failures go it was pretty epic. I can laugh while typing about it now (one-handed obviously) but at the time, if somebody had been snapping candid photographs, they would have captured a whole range of bizarre facial expressions from fright to pain to rage and then to monstrous embarrassment.

If the same photographer had followed me only moments later he would have captured any number of facial expressions from awe to raging envy on the tour of Chateau Stone. Who doesn't envy a bath tub big enough for a rugby team? You could swim laps in this thing it's so huge. And the bubble jets? I have a sneaking suspicion that if you put your head underwater while they're going you'd hear the Hallelujah Chorus in six part harmony. Any and all subsequent photographs would have had me looking like a prune from the hours spent lying in the bath conducting the bubble jet orchestra. Actually the photos of me lying in the bath conducting the orchestra would go a long way towards getting me sectioned and nowhere near the direction of getting me to look photogenic.

Having managed not to freak out my prospective employer with my antics on day one, day two continued with a challenge. I had to write a profile for him for a dating site. I was torn between horror and amusement. I bet that was a pretty weird facial expression. I suspect my lip was curling like a dachshund with a sleep-smooshed face. There might have been a twitch in my eye. Thinking about it now I probably resembled that squirrel from Ice Age except with a dating profile instead of an acorn.

I wrote the profile and, while I think it was successful, I may have come across as the stalker type rather than the observant type when it came to explaining my reasoning. Cue a range of I-swear-I-noticed-them-on-the-tour-and-I-haven't-been-rummaging-under-your-bed/in-your-recycling facial expressions. I don't even want to think what they looked like.

Having developed this theory past a necessary point to prove it, I have now moved on to trying to fix it. I strongly suspect that Botox is the answer. I'm never going to be any less accident-prone and my face is a little like an etch-a-sketch – emotions come and go on it with nary a shake in between. If I had Botox I might assume an expression of 'permanently startled chimp' but it would be an excellent poker face. Yes, if you are wondering, I really did just try and make a face like a startled chimp, further proving my point.

Unfortunately Botox involves the injecting of toxins into my face and I don't think I'm ready for that quite yet. In truth, there's more to life than being photogenic and maybe being this way isn't always bad. My friends know that I am always honest with them because my face totally gives me away when I'm lying. The path of honesty isn't always the easiest but it's certainly the least complicated in the long run and there's a lot to be said for that.

I guess, when it comes right down to it, I'd rather be openly trustworthy than a poker face full of poison. But I would really like the job.

"You are completely nuts but there's no doubt about it – you can blog." Taylor had laughed all the way through reading her writing as they sat at dinner. "Where do you even come up with this stuff? Really? Conducting in the bath?"

"I don't know. I just start writing and the words follow themselves." Elise didn't know whether to feel embarrassed or amused.

"But how did you start with it? I asked you to write about your visit here and the first sentence is about how you're not photogenic. It's the leap of logic that I don't get." He shook his head in amusement. "I'd love to know what life is like from your perspective. Your thought processes must be extraordinary."

"Not really." She could feel herself blushing again. "I just take something from my day and run with it. I go over it in my head before I start writing. I was thinking that your first impression of me probably couldn't have been any worse and that anyone watching it would have thought you were the one that's nuts for still giving me a chance. That naturally progressed to the realisation that anyone watching me through my life would realise I was a hopeless case and that's probably why I don't photograph very well. I'm constantly doing something clumsy or off the wall. That said, I think when it comes to the feature, if I take you up on your offer, I'm sure it'll be about internet dating. That's weird enough all on its own without me having to add any humour."

"Ok, two questions for you." He sat forward in his chair and sipped his wine. "One – why would you consider not taking the job? And two – why were you internet dating in the first place? You're funny and attractive and outgoing. I can't believe you'd have too much trouble finding a guy."

Elise suddenly became very interested in her plate. "It's a big thing to move to London for 3 months or more and it's going to be hard work. I don't know if I've got what it takes to help these guys. What I like might not be what other women are looking for. We also haven't discussed any of the details of it. I know the expenses will be generous to cover the cost of living down there but we still need to hammer out contract details and salary. Anything could go wrong between now and..." She blinked.

"June." Taylor supplied with a smile. "The blog will start in June. I see your point. And question two?"

"I've been single for two and a half years and I live in a tiny village in the middle of nowhere. Apart from the local pub where, let's face it, I'm only going to meet hardened drinkers, there is nowhere to meet guys. There are no evening classes to attend, no clubs to join. I gave up hanging out at the cafe when my jeans started getting too tight from all the cakes I felt duty bound to buy for occupying a table. There's not even a library and I'm not shallow enough to go to church for the sole purpose of meeting men."

"But you've thought about it?" His eyes were twinkling wickedly and Elise burst out laughing.

"It's been a long time. Yeah I thought about it."

He joined her laughing out loud. "You weren't lying about the honesty thing were you?"

"Not at all. But I'll be horribly disappointed if you take advantage of it."

"Oh now! That's not fair! Now that you've said it I'm dying to ask all sorts of questions!" He levelled a steady look at her with a broad grin playing on his lips. "Oh, Elise...that was a foolish thing to say. Now you've done it."

"Okay." Elise set down her knife and fork. "I am going to remind you at this juncture that you want to employ me.

I beg of you not to ask anything that will make our potential working employment awkward."

"I don't know that I can resist the temptation!" He laughed.

"Well you're going to have to." Smiling to cover her unease, Elise got up to take her plate to the kitchen.

"Elise, stop. Look at me." He was aiming for teasing, but there was a darker undertone to it and Elise didn't stop.

"No," she told him firmly, heading for the kitchen. "You're about to cross a line that we can't back over." She pushed through to the kitchen to the relative safety of company.

"You didn't have to bring your plate through," Sam told her with a touch of surprise. "Was everything okay?"

"Yes it was delicious, thank you." Trying to calm the fire in her cheeks, Elise took a deep breath and began to rinse her plate at the sink.

"Ladies, can we have a moment alone please," Taylor said quietly from the doorway and the girls left immediately without a word. "I'm sorry, Elise," he told her sincerely. "Please look at me." Elise rinsed the suds off her hands and turned round to face him. "Why did you run away?" he asked and she sighed.

"You were going to ask me if I found you attractive. I could hear it in your voice. It's in your nature to want to be in a position of control but it's not appropriate to the situation. It would have started out jokingly and ended up as a terrible mess."

"I won't deny that's what I wanted to ask, but I see where you're coming from." He leaned against the door frame. "I don't know what got into me. Actually I do. I find you attractive; I already told you that."

"But you were just being nice at the time," Elise pointed out and he sighed.

"No, actually I wasn't. I find it bizarre that someone as pretty and funny as you has to use a dating website to get a guy. If you weren't so determined to be responsible, I'd be trying really hard to get you into bed right now."

"You told me yesterday you never mixed business with pleasure. I don't think sleeping with your employees is a great way to demonstrate that." She couldn't look at him and grabbed a dish cloth to dry her hands on, twisting it in her fingers. "I know we're not going to see that much of each other, even if I did come to London, but don't you think that a holiday fling would make it a little awkward on the occasions when we do have to meet?"

He seemed amused. "It's just sex! You think we couldn't sleep together and just be friends afterward?"

"Why are you so sure we're going to stay friends?" she protested angrily. He was stirring up all sorts of emotions. "We might as well be on different planets when you look at the social circles we come from. Up here and alone we're getting on fine after 2 days together, but down south, when you're back in your manic office life surrounded by the beautiful people, you won't have time or enthusiasm for a simple country girl like me. I don't have style or polish. I couldn't tell the difference between Versace and Florence and Fred. I don't belong in your world as a friend or as an occasional winter lover whenever you fancy a one night stand. And the fact that you think sex is just sex without any emotional attachment just goes to show what different worlds we come from. I value people too highly to assume I could just use their body when I fancy a tumble, but the world you live in? Even your friends are disposable." She shook her head in disgust. "I'm going to bed. I guess I'll see you at lunch." She stormed out without giving him any chance to defend himself and he stared after her in disbelief.

She took her time coming downstairs the following morning, but he hadn't headed out to the slopes and was waiting for her in the living room, staring moodily out of the window. For a moment she thought about trying to sneak past but then gave up on it.

"I'm sorry about last night," she told him softly. "I said some things I probably shouldn't have said."

"Not at all." He looked like he'd barely slept. "I deserved every word of it and probably a few choice ones that you didn't say. Do you want breakfast?"

"Yes please." She followed him through to the kitchen and they sat at the small table looking out across the hills.

"I feel terrible," he admitted as she slathered jam on a croissant. "You're right about my world in London. It is completely superficial and people are very promiscuous and shallow. I had no right to assume the same about you and I'm ashamed that I did, even for a moment, because you are clearly different." He sighed. "You were more right than you knew when you wrote that profile for me. I do need somebody to challenge me. Last night was a prime example of what I turn into when everybody says yes to me all the time." She opened her mouth to say something, but he hushed her. "No, please let me finish. I do think you're very pretty, Elise, but the more I thought about it overnight, the more I realised that I didn't really want to sleep with you...I was just horny as hell and you were here and I dealt with the situation exactly as I would have done if I had been with some shallow and vacuous bimbo back home instead of an intelligent, charming and funny woman whose friendship I really don't want to lose. And there is the truth of it. We've had such a laugh that when I picture you in my head it's as a friend first and then as a woman. I just don't find you attractive in that way and you stopped me from making a really big mistake last night. I'm hoping that my arrogance and stupidity hasn't totally blown the job offer into smithereens, because I really do think you'd be a great asset to our web team. I'm sorry and I hope you'll forgive me."

"I'll accept the apology and forgive you, but I do need to think about the job," she told him. "It's a big decision."

"I know. I'll send you the paperwork when I get back to the office so you can look it over and take advice on the contract if you need to." He flashed her one of his dazzling smiles and then pulled her into a warm and comfortable hug. "I'm glad we talked this over. I'd quite like to spend many more nights drinking good wine on the balcony playing our guitars."

"Me too. I think I'd like that very much." They squeezed tightly to seal the deal, clinked their coffee cups and the matter was settled.

Taylor left for the airport just after lunch to fly back to London and Elise decided to head straight home. Her wrist was still aching and she hadn't been resting it enough because the swelling was getting worse so she wasn't up to a day out shopping. As it happened it was for the best because her best friend Fern was waiting in her car in Elise's driveway when she pulled into her little hillside cottage.

"How long have you been waiting?" Elise asked as they hugged and Fern shrugged.

"Not long. Maybe only ten minutes or so. I figured you'd leave at the same time as the mysterious Mr Stone so I checked the flight times for London and calculated from there."

"You're far too clever for your own good." Elise laughed. "I'm glad you're here though. Would you carry my bag for me – I broke my wrist and my guitar is in the car too."

"You broke your wrist?" Fern was astonished. "You actually went skiing?"

"No!" Elise blushed. "It's a long story. I'll tell you when we get in. It's bloody freezing out here."

"You get yourself inside and get the kettle on. I'll empty the car. I brought some milk just in case." Fern shooed Elise into the house and brought everything in while

Elise made a pot of tea and opened some biscuits. Then she told her the whole story of the last 3 days from start to finish. Fern's eyes were wide by the time Elise was done. "What are you going to do?" She demanded breathlessly and Elise shrugged.

"I don't know. I mean...it's Monochrome! It's the opportunity of a lifetime. But what if I can't do it? And, if anything, last night just goes to show that it's a totally alien world to me. Do I really want to work for a guy that would sleep with me just because he's horny and I happen to be in the room? I could have been any nameless, faceless woman and that's pretty demeaning."

"I can't believe you turned him down." Fern grinned. "I Googled him. He's gorgeous!"

"He also wants to employ me!" Elise protested, laughing. "It would have been a disaster. Besides, he told me straight up he doesn't think of me romantically. It was an aberration. I'll be astonished if we even stay friends. I'm half convinced he only made the apology this morning because he really wants me to do the feature for him, not because he genuinely likes me. By the time you account for all the hours he spent on the slopes we were only in each other's company for maybe 15 hours and a few of those were spent at the hospital. You mark my words...I won't hear from him again."

Chapter 3

5 weeks later, as she sat on a flight to London, those words came back to haunt Elise. As expected she hadn't heard from Taylor once. Not one word, not a peep, not a single letter, call or email. The paperwork had arrived with a compliment slip scribbled by another of his secretaries and when she had accepted the position and sent everything back it had been Nikki-of-the-perky-voice who organised her flights and accommodation. As much as it had been expected it still stung slightly and Elise didn't know how she would react if she actually saw him in the course of her employment.

She had fully intended not to take the job on at all but one look at the proposed salary and extremely generous contract had forced her to realise that she couldn't afford to turn it down, especially given the clauses that allowed for the term of the contract to be extended to permanent if all went well. She had taken it to a friendly solicitor in town who had looked it over, congratulated her and then taken her to the pub for a bottle of champagne. She'd have been cutting off her nose to spite her face if she'd turned it down because of one silly night where nothing had actually happened.

Nikki met her at the airport and turned out to be just as perky of body as she was of voice and another pang shot through Elise. If he was working with glamorous creatures like this gorgeous sylph-like naiad in front of her then it was no wonder he hadn't called. She glanced down at her own travel rumpled clothes and felt distinctly like the poor cousin. They didn't talk much on the way into the city, although Nikki explained that Elise would be staying in one of Mr Stone's properties.

"How many does he have?" Elise was not really surprised and Nikki shrugged.

"In London or globally?"

"Uh...both?" It really was like landing on a whole other planet.

"In London he has twelve properties personally but he has a few more that he leases to the magazine for exactly this sort of purpose. Globally I'd have to guess at maybe fifty but I'm not really sure. He has a management company that deals with them."

Fifty? Elise shook her head in disbelief and stared out the window at the passing streets. Who needed that many houses? Sure a lot of them would be used for business transactions, but she suspected a lot of them were holiday homes like the chalet in Aviemore. It made her sad to think of all of that gorgeous real estate just lying empty.

Nikki glanced at her with something close to pity on her face. "Look, it's probably not my place to say anything but I feel I should probably tell you, woman to woman...I don't know if anything happened between you and Mr Stone up in Scotland but down here is a completely different ballgame. He goes through women like most people go through clean underwear. They're all wealthy and pretty young socialites. Do you understand what I'm saying?"

Elise willed her face to stop burning at the unintended slight. She knew Nikki was just trying to be kind but it still stung. "I understand. Nothing happened in Scotland. It was just a job interview. I don't sleep with my employers."

"That's good." Nikki nodded and turned her attention back to the traffic and they drove the rest of the way in silence.

The apartment they had put her in was near the wharf. It was a huge modern building all shiny with steel and glass and, although it looked beautiful on the outside, on the inside it was so soulless it made Elise's teeth ache. Her apartment was on the 12th floor and it was fully furnished but, apart from a well stocked kitchen, everything else was empty and the two boxes Elise had shipped down were sitting forlornly in the centre of the palatial living room floor. She parked her suitcase next to them and followed Nikki through to a small study that looked out over the Thames.

"There's a file on here with all the details on the apartment." Nikki gestured to the book shelves. "A cleaner comes once a week and there are local business numbers in there too – taxis and takeaways etc. The local tube station is just up the street if you turn right out the front door. Here are your keys and we keep spares in the office. This is an Oyster card for you." She handed them over. "We've set you up with a company lap top that's linked to the company network. Your email and so on is already set up so you can just click on the office icons. These are the files on the men you will be writing the feature on." She laid a hand on six grey folders sat on the desk by the laptop. "They've all been vetted and are aware of what's going on. I've left names and numbers for all of Mr Stone's secretaries in the rolodex so if you need anything else just give us a call."

"I'm sure I'll be fine." Elise managed a slightly overwhelmed smile. "Just looking forward to getting unpacked and starting work."

"Excellent." Nikki swept up a few items of post on her exit and then Elise was left alone in the echoing flat.

Within half an hour she had unpacked her boxes and suitcase so she grabbed the house file from the study, made a cup of tea in the kitchen with the milk someone had thoughtfully left in the fridge and sat at the breakfast bar to study the folder. As promised there were numbers of taxi companies and takeaway menus but someone had also helpfully printed maps of the area with the nearest post office, grocery store, tube station, hospital and, bizarrely, police station marked in red and green pens. The security code for the wifi was printed neatly alongside the number for the property management company and Elise bookmarked that page for future reference.

With not much else to do and too tired to start looking at the work, Elise finished her tea, took the copy of the map, wrote the address of the apartment in the back of her diary, programmed a taxi number into her phone and left the apartment on foot to go food shopping. It was a beautiful spring day and she took her time meandering into town. It had been a long time since she had last visited London and she had forgotten the constant noise and traffic and heat. With a start she realised she would be able to visit anywhere she wanted in her free time and the thought made her smile. She hadn't been to the Natural History Museum since she was a child and she'd always wanted to visit the V&A. She could go and have dinner in Covent Garden and watch the street performers, perhaps go to a show. She'd always loved musicals and there were probably a few new ones she hadn't seen. With a spring in her step she purchased some breakfast and lunch items and carted them back to her apartment.

When that was done it was still early afternoon so she consulted her map once more, stuck some ID into her purse and set back off out to find the local library. It was in a slightly rundown building that smelled like libraries everywhere – paper, plastic dust covers and cheap carpets. She spent a happy hour perusing the reference books before heading into the fiction section. She hadn't brought anything with her to read and it was one of her favourite pastimes so she selected several books that looked promising and went to register for a card.

"You new here?" The guy behind the counter glanced up and smiled and Elise's breath caught in her throat. He was gorgeous in a nerdy sort of way – brown curls tumbling waywardly all over the place and warm hazel eyes offset by an olive green T-shirt portraying a band Elise had never heard of. "I'm sure I'd remember a face as pretty as yours."

"Yeah I just arrived today." She blushed furiously.

"And you're already in the library checking out..." he glanced at the book at the top of the pile "historical romances? You must be on your own."

Surprised, Elise burst out laughing. "Yeah I'm down here for work for the summer."

"Excellent. Well, we're not really supposed to give out library cards to people who haven't lived here for three months but for you I'll make an exception. Just don't tell anyone." His eyes twinkled. "I might get sacked."

Elise was instantly contrite. "I had no idea. If it'll get you into trouble then don't worry about it. I'll find something else to do."

"Don't worry about it." He waved her concerns away and clacked at the keyboard, entering her name, date of birth and address in. "That is an excellent photograph." He commented as he photocopied her passport for the library records and Elise blushed.

"Thanks. It must have been a lucky day. My last one made me look like a convict."

He burst out laughing. "My current one makes me look like a convict. I don't know how they do it. It must be some function they program into the photo booths." Quickly and efficiently he laminated the card that got printed out and handed it to her with a flourish. "Welcome to London Miss Waterford."

"Thank you." She smiled as he scanned all the books for her and put them into a carrier bag.

"Look," he began as she was about to leave "I know this is pretty forward of me but do you have any friends down here or anyone you know in the city?"

"No. I haven't been here for years and my family lives in the West Country." Elise confessed and he nodded.

"Would you like to go for coffee sometime? I can introduce you to some people, show you the local area. It must be pretty lonely being here on your own."

Elise hesitated but then thoughts of the large empty apartment awaiting her at the wharf surfaced and she smiled. "Are you sure? That would be great."

"Of course I'm sure." He fished around in his pockets and produced a slightly battered mobile phone. "What's your number?" Elise recited it to him and he programmed it in, calling it once he had it saved, and Elise could feel her phone buzzing about in her bag. "Now you have my number too. My name is Nathan." He stuck out his hand and Elise shook it, smiling so widely she thought her face might crack.

"Elise. Nice to meet you."

"You too. Pretty name." He grinned. "I'm off work tomorrow so I'll call in the morning and we can arrange somewhere to meet."

"I look forward to it." Still smiling she headed back out into the crisp spring sunshine and headed back to the apartment with a feeling that the summer might not be so bad after all.

She slept well and was in the study by 10am checking emails and flicking through the folders they had left for her. Everything seemed fairly straightforward and she had several emails from people introducing themselves and explaining the procedures to her. There was still nothing from Taylor which she found a little odd, given that he was now the overall editor of the section she would be working on and therefore her line manager, but Nikki's words replayed themselves in her head and she sighed. Of course he didn't have time for the likes of her.

Nathan called just before lunch and they arranged to meet at a small independent coffee house about half an hour's walk from the apartment. It was another sunny day so Elise walked there enjoying the sights and sounds of the big city. He was just as cute as she'd remembered him and turned out to be surprisingly funny and charming for someone who was so clearly a geek. They laughed all afternoon talking about their backgrounds and hobbies and why Elise was in the city. At six o'clock when they were clearly waiting to close the cafe Nathan took her hand.

"Come on, I don't think we've finished this conversation yet. We'll have to move on to dinner!" Laughingly Elise agreed and they headed to the tube station. An hour and several changes later they had travelled on the northern line to Colindale and disembarked.

"I've never been to this part of London before." Elise looked around at the industrial buildings and housing estates and Nathan grinned.

"Not many people have but it's the home of the best Chinese food in the city. There's a big Chinese shopping mall here, the Yaohin Plaza. It's a bit of a walk though. Do you want to get a taxi?"

"No, I'm fine walking." So they strolled hand in hand through the streets while Nathan told her about the other sights in the area. The Air Force museum was in Colindale as well as the headquarters for the Health Protection Agency. Elise was beginning to realise how valuable it was to have a friend who knew the city. She'd never have found this place on her own.

By the time they got to the mall most of the shops were closed but the food courts, restaurants and Chinese food markets were doing a roaring trade and they finally settled at a table with trays stuffed to bursting with freshly cooked food.

"This is amazing!" Elise didn't know where to start. She had scallops in oyster sauce with cashew nuts, beef strips on black bean sauce, noodles and two different kinds of rice. Nathan had encouraged her to try some of everything and his plate was no less stuffed.

"I would say it's a good idea to start from the outside and work in." He advised wisely and she grinned.

"Excellent plan. Don't expect any conversation for at least twenty minutes."

He was already tucking in to his. "Girl, you are going to get no arguments from me!"

It was after ten o'clock by the time they arrived back at her apartment. Nathan had insisted on walking her back to the door saying it wasn't safe for a girl to be out on the streets on her own but there wasn't any awkwardness as they arrived.

"Thank you for a lovely evening!" He announced gallantly, kissing her cheek. "Well, day really considering what time we started."

"No, thank *you*. I've had a great time." Elise grinned at him and he bowed.

"Excellent. I'm going to a barbecue tomorrow night if you want to come. It's going to be a big group of my friends so it won't be awkward. We might even go out afterwards." Elise hesitated and he did the most amazing puppy dog eyes she'd ever seen on a human. "Please say you'll come, it'll be a laugh."

"Okay, I'll come." She found herself saying and he grinned broadly, flashing strong white teeth.

"Awesome. I'll meet you at the tube station at six?"

"Okay." She let him kiss her cheek again and then he was away, striding down the street on long, lean legs with a bounce in his step. Chuckling, Elise went into the building and headed upstairs to bed with her cheeks aching from smiling too much.

She slept late the following morning and spent most of the day in her pyjamas going over the files for the men she referred to in her head as 'the projects'. There wasn't much detail on them and she could totally understand why none of them had been particularly successful at internet dating. Their profiles were so bland you could have wallpapered with them. She had to be honest and admit that if she had seen them on a dating site she probably wouldn't have contacted them. It was actually quite depressing. Somehow she had to turn this around and make them desirable, or at the very least interesting. Starting back from the beginning she put them in the order she wanted to deal with them and then started calling to make arrangements to meet.

She met Nathan at the station at six o'clock as promised and the moment he saw her his face lit up in a way that made her stomach fill with butterflies. She couldn't believe her luck bumping into him on the first day in the city. It was enough to make her believe that everything happened for a reason and sometimes things are just meant to be.

They started making their way towards Wimbledon where his friends lived and Elise checked her outfit nervously. He had said not to dress up and he himself looked casual in jeans and yet another band top but she had wanted to make a good impression and was wearing a cute sweater with her jeans.

"Stop worrying, you look beautiful." He said as they flew past another station in a blur of bright lights and faces.

She snorted. "Not sure about beautiful but thanks for the sentiment. Do they know I'm coming?"

"Yeah I called this morning." He grinned. "They're looking forward to meeting you but my brother will be there so don't be surprised if he teases you."

"Thanks for the warning." She swatted his arm playfully. "I'm sure I'll be fine."

"I know you will be. Just give as good as you get." He winked at her and took her hand as they left the train, leading her up the steps and out into the sunlight. "This way, it's not far." The house was only a five minute walk from the station and the front door was open. Nathan squeezed her hand reassuringly and led her up the front steps straight into the house. "Hello?" He called loudly.

"We're out back!" Yelled a female voice and Nathan led Elise through a hallway and a kitchen and back out into the sunshine into a fairly small garden that seemed to be crammed with people. There was a flurry of fist-bumping, arm clasping and laughing and then Elise wanted the ground to open up and swallow her whole as everyone stepped back and stared curiously at her.

"So this is library girl." It had to be Nathan's brother – they had the same hair and eyes.

"And this must be Nathan's brother." She stuck her hand out, smiling. "Elise."

"Harry. Nice to meet you." He shook her hand and she realised he also had Nathan's dazzling smile. "Did he really pick you up at the library?"

"He didn't pick me up." Elise winked at Nathan. "He came to my rescue like a knight in shining armour. I was the damsel in distress. It was my first day and I didn't know anyone."

"That's my boy." Harry bumped knuckles with Nathan and then put his arm around Elise, scooping her away from his brother. "Come with me and I'll introduce you round."

Nathan had been right – his friends were great and the food was delicious. By the time they staggered out in the direction of the bar she already had four new numbers in her mobile memory and plans to meet up with the girls for coffee on Sunday afternoon. She was practically floating down the street, semi-convinced that if Nathan wasn't holding her hand she might have taken off.

"So, you and my brother an item?" Harry said in her ear under the music as Nathan headed for the bar and Elise shrugged, blushing.

"I only met him the day before yesterday!" She protested. "Give us some time!"

"Tell me he's at least made his intentions clear?" He sounded mocking and Elise swatted him.

"He's been a perfect gentleman. Which is more than I can say for you."

"Hey!" He looked wounded but the twinkle in his eyes gave him away. "I just want to know if I stand a chance! If he's claimed dibs then I'll back off but if you're just friends I'd like to take you out some time."

"Oh that's low!" Nathan's friend Amanda had overheard and butted in. "You wait 'til your little brother's buying you a drink and then you try and steal his girl?"

"I ain't stealing anything!" Harry laughed. "I was just clarifying the situation!"

"What situation?" Nathan was back from the bar and Elise went bright red when everyone laughed.

"Harry was putting the moves on your girl." Amanda declared.

"I wasn't!" Harry protested. "I was just finding out if she *is* your girl. I wasn't sure. Is she your girl?"

Nathan blinked. "Uh...Hold on." He held up a finger and then vanished into the crowd.

"Where's he going?" Harry was just as bemused as everyone else but Amanda stood on her chair and scanned the crowd.

"He's talking to the DJ!" She yelled down to the table.

"Oh no." Elise put her head into her hands. Talking to the DJ could only mean bad things. Very public bad things.

The song came to an end and the DJ flicked on his mic. "Well tonight ladies and gentleman we have a special request, especially for the girl in the cute red sweater at that table over there." Everyone scanned the table and Elise shrank low in her seat as the group burst out laughing. "I think you'll give the guy a round of applause for this *inspired* choice of track."

There was a base guitar line and then a very distinctive guitar riff before the lyrics started and Amanda creased, clearly recognising the song. "Oh my God, I have GOT to film this!" She hauled her phone out of her bag and pointed it at the crowd, scanning for Nathan. And then he appeared. Elise laughed so much she thought her sides were going to cave in. He was rocking out old school as he came in her general direction, cosied right up to her and yelled along with the lyrics:

"...big black boots and her long brown hair..." he flicked her hair with a wink "...she's so cute with that GET BACK STARE!" He flung himself away dramatically as the crowd whistled and cheered. "Now I can see you home with me, but you were with another maaaaaan yeah!" He pointed at Harry and the crowd obediently booed and gestured. "I know we ain't got much to say before I let you get away yeah! I said are you gonna be my girl?" He held his hand out, beckoning her to come to him and, despite herself, Elise got up and took it. He pulled her in right close and sang the next lyrics. "I said one two three take my hand and come with me because you look so fine that I really want to make you mine. I said you look so fine that I really wanna make you mine." He pulled her back towards the dance floor and Elise was giggling so much she could barely keep upright.

"You're crazy!" She called over the music as the crowd pressed in around them cheering along and dancing to the music.

"Just dance with me!" He called back. And so she did.

They caught the last train home, still giggling as they left their friends in Wimbledon, hugging every last one of them thoroughly.

"That was so much fun!" Elise laughed as they arrived at the door to her apartment building. "Thank you so much!"

"For what? Taking you out?" He grinned at her.

"For everything! For introducing me to people, for taking me out, for that crazy-ass stunt you pulled at the club...all of it."

"Well, it seemed kind of appropriate at the time." He chuckled. "I'm never going to listen to that track in the same way again."

"Me either. And you are one hell of a dancer!" She did a little shimmy up against him. "The geek got moooooves."

"I like to dance." He shrugged. "Maybe we should go to a class or something. I bet you'd do an excellent tango." He pulled her into hold and marched her halfway down the street and back as she howled with laughter and tried not to trip over her feet.

"Oh my god, stop!" She panted as they got to the door again and he did a head flick. "My sides hurt!"

"I'm sorry." He wasn't really and they both knew it but he obediently dropped her arms and placed his hands on her hips, gently massaging her sides.

"You're kind of tall." Elise looked up at him and he grinned.

"You're not. You're tiny and perfectly formed." He leaned down and kissed her tentatively on the mouth. "Is this okay?" He whispered and she smiled against his lips.

"It's better than okay."

He kissed her again, this time with a fierceness that took her breath away and left her legs wobbling, his tongue dancing with hers as her fingers tangled in his hair.

"Do you want to come up?" She whispered shyly when he released her and his eyes went liquid with want.

"I'd better not." His voice was ragged. "I have a three date rule."

"Technically we did coffee and dinner yesterday." She pointed out. "Plus tonight that makes three."

"That's cheating." He kissed her again and then rested his forehead against hers. "Right now we're both high on life and we've had a few drinks. I really don't want to mess this up and do something either of us regrets."

"Then come for dinner tomorrow." She suggested. "I have to go into the office in the afternoon for an hour or so but I'll stop at the shop on the way home and get something to cook for us."

"Excellent plan." He sighed. "God I really hope you still feel like this tomorrow."

"I'm pretty sure I will." She cupped his cheeks in her palms and kissed him gently. "I'll look forward to it."

"Good." He groaned and pulled himself away from her. "I have to go before I change my mind and haul you upstairs like some sort of caveman. Sleep well and I'll see you tomorrow."

"You too." She blew him a kiss and bounced through the door of the apartment building, too excited to wait for the lift and bounding up the stairs two at a time. It had been one of the best nights of her life.

Chapter 4

The following afternoon Elise stopped by the office and let them give her a make-over for the picture that would go in her byline. She felt awkward posing for it but when they brought the pictures up on the screen they didn't look too gawky and when they inserted the best one into the page layout they had planned for the feature it was hardly noticeable. They described where the words and pictures were going to go, both in the magazine and on the site, and they also showed her the layouts they had been designing for her blog. For the first time Elise began to get a sense that this was all real and it was quite a daunting prospect but they assured her that she would do just fine and eventually she left the office feeling a little more confident.

The sun just about blinded her as she headed into the street and she didn't shade her eyes quickly enough to see the man she walked into.

"Fuck! I'm so sorry!" She winced and shielded her eyes to look up. "Oh! Hi Taylor! How are you?" She knew she was grinning warmly but he didn't look particularly happy to see her.

"Elise." He greeted coolly. "This is turning into a habit, you swearing at me."

She flushed beet red. "I'm so sorry. At least this time I won't break anything or accuse you of sneaking up on me. I was blinded by the sun. Did I hurt you?"

"Not at all. Enjoy your afternoon." And just like that he was gone, sweeping past her with his entourage of beautiful people. Elise felt about an inch tall. Something had happened in between now and the last time they met that had really pissed him off but she was damned if she knew what it was. Shaking it off she reminded herself of the night ahead and headed for the shops leaving thoughts of Taylor behind her.

By the time the buzzer went on her apartment door she was almost finished making the lasagne. "Come on up." She said into the phone, pressing the lock. "The door is open." She propped the door of the apartment open and went back to the kitchen to start on the salad.

"You can tell you don't live in the city!" Nathan told her reprovingly from behind a giant bunch of flowers. "You didn't wait for me to say hi before you opened the door. I could have been a murderer."

"I haven't been here long enough to upset anyone." She grinned, accepting the flowers and searching for a vase. Giving up she propped them in a jug she found in a cupboard. "I know it's not very classy. I'll buy a vase tomorrow if I don't find one somewhere. They're beautiful, thank you."

"No problem." He kissed her cheek and she inhaled his warm scent.

"You smell really good." She stepped back. "You're looking pretty fine too." And she meant it. Some guys could rock a leather jacket and Nathan was clearly one of them. "Let me take your coat – there's a cupboard in the hall." He let her take it and when she returned he was leaning up against the worktop.

"Dinner smells great." He smiled. "Are we having lasagne?"

"Yes it's in the oven. Is that okay?"

"It's my favourite." He patted his tummy. "Especially when it's homemade."

"No jars in my kitchen!" Elise laughed. "How was work?"

"Awful." He grimaced and she gasped.

"Really? Oh no! What happened?"

"It wasn't really awful." He chuckled. "I was just angling for a hug." He held his arms out and she stepped into them, laughing.

"You could have just asked." She grumbled jokingly. "I really thought you'd had a bad day."

"I'm sorry. Next time I'll just ask. Or I'll sneak up on you and steal one before you realise that's where I'm headed."

"Stealth hugs huh?" She leaned up against the full length of him as his arms closed around her. "I think I can live with that."

"Good." They stood in comfortable silence for a moment or two and then Elise sighed.

"I should get the salad ready." She tried to push away but he tightened his arms.

"Nope. By my calculations I've spent a whole 19 hours away from you so I don't think we've done nearly enough cuddling yet." He joked. "How long before the lasagne comes out?"

"Um, about twenty-five minutes." She was too amused to be cross.

"Then we have a whole fifteen minutes to cuddle in and I'll help you make the salad." He declared and Elise relaxed back into him.

"Fine. But if it's burnt it's totally your fault."

"I will accept that responsibility." He planted a kiss on her forehead. "How was your day?"

"It was okay. Having my photo done was awkward but they showed me what the site is going to look like and it's pretty cool."

"That's good." He shifted slightly, settling comfortably against the granite. "So, about last night..."

Elise snuggled into his chest. "I hope you're about to tell me that you still feel that way without being under the influence...?"

He relaxed almost imperceptibly. "Yeah, I do. Do you?"

"Definitely. I kinda like you Nathan Redwood."

She could sense him grinning. "Just 'kinda'?"

"Well it's part like, part lust and part butterflies. It all amounts to like with a little..." she searched for the word "...torque?"

"Excellent. Because I've been dying to do this since I walked through the door." He tilted her chin and leaned down to kiss her, gently at first and then with a breathless urgency as she responded.

They spent most of Saturday in the bedroom fooling around and catching up on sleep, watching movies together and eating too much ice cream. Elise couldn't remember the last time she'd laughed so much. She'd perched on a chair with her guitar and sung to him until he thought his heart was going to burst. By the time Sunday came around neither of them particularly wanted to go out and face the real world but they were running low on food and Elise had promised the girls she'd meet up with them. She couldn't rely on Nathan to fill her world. She needed friends. In the end they agreed she would go for coffee and he would go to the shop. He had to stop at home to get clean clothes so he'd pick her up on the way back to hers and they'd cook a Sunday roast together.

Like most good plans it didn't stick to schedule. Elise and the girls had so much fun in town that by the time Nathan arrived they persuaded him to stay and ordered another round of coffees and before they knew what was happening all the girls had been invited back for dinner as well. Elise was torn between wishing she and Nathan were alone and being overjoyed that the huge echoing apartment was full of laughter and warmth and home cooking smells.

In the end she went to bed with a smile on her face and a man in her arms, feeling that all was right with the world.

On Monday morning Nathan woke her with a cup of coffee and a kiss before he rushed out to work and she drank it in bed feeling very pleased with herself. At 9 o'clock she got up and had a shower and by half ten she was at her desk ready to face the world. She'd decided to blog on Mondays, Wednesdays and Fridays and they had to have it by 3pm at the latest on that day so that it could go through the editing process before being posted online at 7pm.

Tomorrow I am going to meet the first of my 'projects'. His name is Mark and I know absolutely nothing about him other than that he likes watching rugby and lives in London. His photo is very quirky and interesting but doesn't actually show him. I'm not sure if he's trying to be an enigma or if he really doesn't have a clue that women would find this off-putting.

I find I'm quite nervous about this whole concept. What if I meet him and discover that there is absolutely nothing likeable about him? I'll be like the marketing people that put labels on blueberries. (Bossy voice: Come on guys!! It's a super-food!! It HAS to have more than one instruction!! Minion voice: I have an idea boss! Let's tell people they need to eat them at room temperature because it improves the flavour! No-one will ever know...). Will I find myself drowning in a sea of fibs by omission in an attempt to make him look good or will he turn out to have some hidden desirable feature? Like being a superhero. Or rescuing kittens. Or running a charity for kids that have nothing. Would it be weird to ask him to take his shirt off so I can a) check if he's wearing a spandex bodysuit underneath, or b) try and picture a kitten snuggled up to his pectoral?

I am also fretting about the diplomacy issue. The truth is I'm painfully honest and when I say painful I really mean it. If he turns up in an orange shirt and asks me if it looks good I'm going to tell him straight up he resembles a shrink-wrapped chorizo. I am extremely liable to tell the unwashed that they need to shower down because their hair is starting to resemble seaweed. Worse, I may ask a man with halitosis to open wide so the coroner can back his van in to remove whatever's decomposing. I am hoping against hope that he has none of these issues or myriad others that could lead me to say something massively offensive on my mission to change his world. That would be bad.

I also find I really want to help these men. Having been on my own for almost three years I know how it feels to be crushed by loneliness. I have spent my fair share of days in my pyjamas and onesie (sexy I know) crying into a carton of Ben and Jerry's (even sexier – snot is SUCH a good look on me...) because I miss being held. Of all the things I missed most about having a guy in my life it wasn't the talking or the company, it was that quiet hour when you're lying in bed, halfway between waking and sleeping, when the world is hushed and dark and your man has his arms around you and right then, right there, it's the safest and warmest place on earth. I firmly believe it's intrinsically tied in to a woman's self-worth. Being held as though you are a precious item, a porcelain doll, an unwrapped Easter egg...it makes you FEEL precious.

I assume (possibly wrongly) that the reverse is true for men. I wonder if holding a woman in their arms makes them feel they have something of worth in their life and therefore they are worthy by default? I suspect it makes them feel manly. This here is my woman and I will defend her against all takers because I AM MAN, hear me roar. Cue gorilla-like beating of chests and the firm belief that a spray of Lynx will indeed be the siren call to all those beauties. To not have a woman, then, does this make men feel lonely *and emasculated? Would they admit it if it did? How deep do I need to dig into the psychology of this to help these guys? Are we talking just the 6 feet required to exhume and resurrect their mojo or are we going all the way to China to turn their worlds upside down?*

Only one way to find out. Roll on tomorrow and Project 1.

Elise spent a few moments tidying up the grammar and editing some of the sentences before spending a subsequent half hour agonising over every word in case they thought it was too crazy or totally unfunny. She went and had a long lunch and then came back to it but there was nothing else to write at this early stage so eventually she bit the bullet and attached it to an email, pressing send before she could change her mind and screw herself up about it anymore.

She tried to watch some tv while she waited for a response but was too nervous and ended up pacing restlessly about the apartment. Her inbox finally pinged at half past six and she rushed to the computer to open the email. It was from Taylor and all it had was two words: "It's fine."

She slumped in her chair deflated. She wasn't sure what she had been expecting but at the very least it had involved constructive criticism. And 'fine' wasn't exactly a resounding endorsement of her work. Her cursor hovered over the reply button but she didn't know what to say or even where to start. He was totally different here to how he was in Scotland and, even given her reservations about his reasons for apologising, she just couldn't believe he could be such a totally different person. Her phone rang and, looking at the caller ID, she felt her worries melting away. Nathan was obviously home from work and as she answered the phone she shut her lap top and ignored the email from her boss. Life was too short to worry about someone so obviously shallow.

The following morning she got up bright and early and chose her outfit carefully. Nothing too casual but nothing too business-like either. She wanted this man to be relaxed in her company so he would open up to her. They met at mid-morning in a coffee shop not far from his house and it wasn't anywhere near as bad as she had been expecting.

Sure he wasn't all that in the looks department but he was wearing a very dapper and plainly expensive business suit that made the most of what he had. Unfortunately that was where the positives ended. It seemed his internet dating experiences had made him eminently bitter.

"I'm tired of it." He complained. "I'm tired of the rejections and the snooty girls who send you one email and then you never hear from them again. It's plain rude. I keep meaning to delete my profile but then they called me about you and I figured it couldn't be any worse than what I've already been through. But this is it. Once I've done this I am through with internet dating."

He continued in the same vein for the entire duration of their coffee house visit and, despite her best attempts to get him to open up about himself, Elise left the cafe with him knowing nothing more than she had when they'd arrived. She had discovered he was in banking but although it made him a lot of money it wasn't a job he was happy in. He just did it to pay the bills. To hear him talk about it he didn't do anything with his free time and his group of friends was limited to other wealthy bachelors who spent a lot of time drinking and playing poker. It was depressing.

In an effort to learn more about him Elise asked if she could visit his home. He agreed and they walked up the street and round the corner into a leafy suburb with large townhouses set back from the road.

"This is a beautiful area." She commented politely as he pushed through a gate and walked up a pathway through a very bland front garden. To her astonishment he actually showed some enthusiasm.

"It is and it changes every season. In autumn the leaves go the most amazing colours and sometimes in the winter when we get snow it's like going back in time. Check out that old Victorian lamppost!" He let them in the front door and went to hang his jacket up. "Go take a look around." He called back to her. "Would you like a drink?"

"A glass of water would be lovely thanks!" She called back and wandered from the hallway through into a beautifully appointed living room. It was tastefully decorated in shades of grey and it should have been cold but it wasn't. A massive bay window at one end of the room filled it with light and the colours totally complimented a range of black and white photographs that were displayed all around the walls.

Stepping up for a closer look Elise was impressed – they had clearly been chosen by someone with an interest in art and humanity. "These are beautiful!" She told him when he came back into the room with her water. "Where did you get them from?"

He suddenly looked awkward. "Well, that one I took in Thailand..."

For a brief moment yesterday morning I thought I was doomed to fail. I met Mark, my Project 1, for coffee and for a whole hour I battered pointlessly at his barriers, trying to get through to see the man underneath. I failed. I was torn between a mildly misplaced anger at him for refusing to help himself and a weird kind of sad rage at the people who had made him so. He was so down on himself I almost suggested that counselling might be more appropriate than dating. Almost.

In a last ditch attempt to find out something about him I suggested he take me to see his house. It made me realise even more why he has been such a failure on the dating front. No sane or self-respecting woman would take on such a monstrous mothering project by doing something so utterly unsafe as visiting a total stranger's home on the first date unless she was having a moment of madness. Or she was doing a feature on it. I didn't have any choice but to persist.

Imagine my astonishment when I walk through the front door and everywhere in the house are these incredible photographs. I instantly assume that he has purchased National Geographic prints or they are from some famous photographer and he is amassing an heirloom collection. More out of fascination than politeness (because I just <u>knew</u> I wouldn't be able to afford them) I asked him where he got them from and just about died of shock when he admitted he had taken them. These incredible photographs...every one of them was his and each came with a story.

I was utterly floored. I didn't know whether to sing the Hallelujah chorus, weep for joy that there was finally something I could use or lambast him for being such an idiot. In that moment he was transformed in my eyes into one of the most astonishing people I have ever met.

I look at him and it makes my heart swell. I firmly believe that anyone who can see such beauty in the ordinary, who can look at the heart of a thing and see how <u>extraordinary</u> it is, no matter how ugly on the outside, must have such a well of beauty within themselves that to see the world through their eyes must be both dazzling and humbling. I found my mind whispering poetry within itself about seeing the world in a grain of sand. If I were a religious person I would say that he showed me the hand of God moving in all His creations. His pictures are taken with *a sweet innocence that strips down everything he photographs to its soul and leaves the viewer's heart aching with awe. It was an incredible experience.*

When I asked him why he had not mentioned his photography in his profile, or indeed his far-reaching and extensive passion for travelling, he looked around at the pictures and his shoulders slumped. He said he'd been told they weren't very good. It turns out that he has never had training and in the hopes of achieving some constructive criticism he had put one or two of his favourite pictures onto an online photography forum. They had been roundly and thoroughly rubbished by a group of snobbish, perfectionist and soulless idiots interested in nothing but preserving their own careers and reputations. It seemed to me that in looking for the minutiae they had totally missed the raw and breathtaking power of the whole.

I was raging and in that moment I realised that I wanted to defend this man. I wanted to promote him, befriend him, be there for him and find him happiness because some deep part of me was inspired by him. He has shown me, in more ways than one, that a book should never be judged by its cover. I am ashamed now of the time I spent thinking him bland and a failure and I have learned a valuable lesson today. For that I will always be grateful.

So I have my starting point for reconstruction – I am taking a real photographer with nothing to lose to his house to see his pictures and who can give him an honest opinion of his works. I have also allocated him homework – he has to write me a list of his top ten favourite countries to visit and why. He has to give me opinions on the languages and foods as well as the culture and history. It'll be interesting to see what he comes up with. I suspect I may be surprised.

If I can get him to have some faith in himself then, ladies and gents, I believe we are onto a winner.

Elise typed the last line, read it through once and then attached it to an email, sending it off without a second thought. As it vanished from her outbox she called the office directly and requested to speak to the photography department. After almost half an hour of transferred calls and negotiations she had herself a professional photographer who had been in the field for years who was prepared to take some time out of his day the next day to come with her to Mark's house to appraise his photographs.

That settled she was wondering what to do next when the buzzer rang. Picking up the phone by the door she said hello and burst out laughing when she discovered it was Nathan pretending to be a pizza delivery guy. She let him up and they sat at the breakfast bar in the kitchen demolishing pizza with a couple of glasses of red wine.

He told her about his day at the library, which had been surprisingly action-packed, and then asked how her day had gone. She told him all about Mark, all about the pictures and how she planned to try and make him have a little more faith in himself. He made her read him her blog entry and then he took her to bed.

After they had made love he held her in his arms, stroking her hair absently with one hand as they lay in the darkness and silence. When his hand stilled she thought he had gone to sleep but then he let out a deep breath.

"You're a dangerous woman Elise Waterford." He said softly. "You were right about how being able to see something beautiful in the ordinary makes you beautiful within yourself but I don't think you realise how the same applies to you."

The next day Elise turned up on Mark's doorstep with the photographer at 10am. He was home having taken the week off work for the feature and he looked nervous as he invited them in. Elise was hoping and praying that her gamble was going to pay off and wouldn't push him even further into his pit of self-hatred but she needn't have worried.

The photographer, confusingly also called Mark, stopped dead in the middle of the living room and his eyes widened as he turned on the spot, scanning the walls as he took in the pictures. Elise touched a finger to her lips and pulled Project 1 out of the way so the photographer could absorb the full effect. Project 1 clearly had no idea how spectacular the impact of his pictures as a collection was and he watched in confusion as the photographer turned on the spot gazing at each picture in turn. He did a full three rounds of the room before he turned back to them. His face was a little pale.

"You took all of these yourself?" He asked faintly and Project 1 nodded.

"Not all with the same camera or in the same country but yeah, they're all mine."

"And you've had no training?" There was an element of disbelief in the photographer's voice and Elise could see project 1 was getting defensive.

"Only a few things I read on the internet. I know I've got to improve but-"

"They're incredible." The photographer shook his head and project 1 was, for the moment, shocked into silence. "Journalists win Pulitzers with photographs like these." He gaped at Elise's favourite picture of a young boy emerging from the sea. Small droplets of water rested on his eye lashes like tiny jewels and the water streaming on his skin gave him a weirdly ethereal luminescent look. "I've seen National Geographic pictures that aren't this good." They waited in silence while he did another full turn of the room and then Elise took control.

"If he wanted to learn more about the technique, where would he go and what would he do?" She asked and the photographer focused on her slowly.

"I can recommend some excellent technical courses, but the truth is I think we should pitch to a gallery." He looked at Mark. "Would you like to come visit my studio?"

"What do you mean pitch to a gallery?" Elise asked before Project 1 could answer.

"He's got a gift." The photographer shrugged. "It's not just the taking of the pictures or the pictures themselves...it's the collection, the way they're presented, the way they take your breath away when you walk into the room. Couldn't you see an exhibition of these in a gallery?" His face lit up with enthusiasm. "Imagine a series of smaller ones like these and maybe a couple blown up onto canvas sized glossy." Elise struggled to picture it in her head and the photographer sighed. "Have you ever bought a professional photograph?" He asked, clearly trying a different tack, and she shook her head. "Okay, if you had to guess, how much would you pay for one of these pictures?"

At that Elise had to grin. "That was one of the first things I thought when I saw them yesterday, that I wouldn't be able to afford them."

"Well there you are." He turned to project 1. "How many pictures do you have? Have you got a portfolio?"

Project 1 looked embarrassed. "No I haven't. I've got lots more though. These are my favourites but I have a few up in every room." That took them on a tour of the house. They looked at photographs for almost an hour and Elise didn't even get bored. Each room was like a new adventure.

When they finally made it back to the living room the photographer turned to project 1. "How do you store these? Are they digital or old-school?"

"A mix of both." Project 1 shrugged. "When I started I was using film. Now I mostly go digital unless it's for a special project."

The photographer scratched his head and shook his shoulders out. "Look, this might seem a little presumptuous of me but my studio does consulting in various photographical fields. If you were prepared to pay us a consultancy fee and bring everything you have in we'll help you get set up with a proper portfolio of your work and then our agents can work on pitching them to galleries and publications. Is that something you'd be interested in?"

Project 1 was astonished. "I'd love to! Obviously we'd have to figure out details and costs but yes...that's definitely something I'd be interested in."

"Great." The photographer pulled a business card out of his pocket, scribbled his mobile number on the back and handed it to project 1. "I'm out all afternoon but I'll be in the studio tomorrow. Call me first thing on any of these numbers to work out the small print and I might be able to fit you in for a couple of hours tomorrow afternoon."

"I will." Project 1 accepted the business card and the photographer left. When the door was closed, Mark turned to Elise with the hugest grin on his face and she pointed at it.

"You see this face? This is what I want to see more of, you hear me? Now, go and get the homework I set you and the proper work will begin..."

"Yes ma'am!" Still smiling he went to find his notes and behind his back Elise silently punched the air in glee. She could do this. She was going to get this man a date if it killed her.

Chapter 5

When Elise got home that night after a busy afternoon going over all of Mark's hidden talents and writing copious notes for the profile they were going to create on Friday she was exhausted and decided she wanted nothing better than to have a long soak in the bath. Nathan wasn't coming over because he had stuff to do so she put some music on, ran a bath, shucked off her clothes and climbed gratefully into the tub with one of her borrowed books to relax for a couple of hours, topping up the water every time the temperature dropped. It was blissful.

Because she'd done her blog post for that evening the night before she nearly didn't even switch her computer on when she towelled off and put her pyjamas on but then she realised she hadn't had an email about it and if there were edits she would totally have missed the deadline. She swore. Loudly. Luckily there weren't any edits but the email she had from Taylor was just as confusing.

Dear Elise, he said, *I was surprised to read your blog post. Were his pictures really that good? Seems to be going well. Glad you've taken to it so naturally. Taylor x*

There was a kiss. What the hell did that mean? He'd gone from nothing, to barely civil, to suddenly sentences of more than two words followed by a kiss. The phone rang as she frowned at the screen and she picked it up, barely looking at the screen before she answered.

"Hey beautiful lady!" Nathan sounded tired but cheerful. "How did your day go? Was the photographer a success?"

"Definitely." The memory made her smile. "Turns out it wasn't just me – he was so impressed he's taking

Mark to his studio to build a portfolio tomorrow. They're going to pitch to a gallery for an exhibition of his work. I knew it was special!"

"That's excellent news! I'm so pleased for you but even more for him. He must be delighted."

"Yeah he is." Elise closed the laptop without drafting a response to the email. Taylor could wait until tomorrow. She didn't need the headache right now. She just wanted to laugh with Nathan and get an early night. "How was your day?"

"Nothing special but I was good when I got home and did all my chores." He sighed. "We've been invited to my mum's for dinner on Saturday. You up for that or is that just a little too scary at this early stage in our relationship?"

"We've been invited or you've been invited?" Elise asked curiously and he burst out laughing.

"We. Harry got straight on the phone to my mum the morning after the barbecue. She's tamping that I didn't tell her about you myself."

"But we weren't even together then!" Elise protested, amused despite herself. "You surely don't tell her about relationships that don't exist?"

"That's what I told her." He started to laugh. "That was when she started shouting at me for not telling her on Sunday after we did get together."

"She shouted at you?" Elise was torn between trying not to giggle and being horrified.

"Well...not really." He conceded. "But she was hurt. So we need to make nice. She's the cream in the centre of my family's Victoria sponge. You don't want her to go off...ruins the whole cake."

"She's the cream in the family cake?" Elise couldn't help it, she snorted with laughter and then burst into outright laughing. "That's a good one. I might have to use it."

"Be my guest." He sounded pleased. "So yes or no? I need to call her back tonight and let her know."

"Yes okay, I'll go with you. Just let me know times and things and I'll be there with bells on."

"Excellent."

On Thursday morning Elise sat at her computer and stared again at the email from Taylor. She wasn't meeting Mark until 10am so she really did need to send some sort of response before she left the apartment or Taylor might think she had spurned his peace offering. If indeed a peace offering is what it was.

After a good fifteen minutes of staring at the screen she got angry with herself and clicked the reply button.

Thanks Taylor. Yes, his pictures really are that good. The photographer I took yesterday thought so too. One day when Mark wins a Pulitzer you'll be able to say with pride that it was Monochrome who discovered him. I'm feeling pretty hopeful that we'll get him a date but we shall see. Elise

Her hand hovered over the x. To kiss or not to kiss? That was indeed the question. Adding one in response to his seemed the polite thing to do but what if he had switched personalities again overnight and wasn't feeling as magnanimous as he had the day before? It was at times like this that you needed a rule book for male-female correspondence issues. The Idiots Guide to Talking to Guys.

After another fifteen minutes of vacillating between staring at the x and staring at the screen she got annoyed with herself all over again and hit the full stop, clicking send on the email. She reasoned that any guy who blew hot and cold all the time needed to learn not to treat women that way. She wasn't going to be affectionate until such time as he provided a reasonable explanation for his behaviour. She was not some door mat to be picked up and put down as he saw fit. Feeling empowered and righteous she grabbed her shoes and bag and left the apartment ready for her meeting with Mark.

He was full of excitement and anticipation for his afternoon at the photography studio. He confessed he'd been up for a large portion of the night digging out negatives and flash drives with his photographs on to contribute to his portfolio and he'd organised to head in at 2pm. Since that only left them 3 hours together at most, given that he had to travel to get to the studio, Elise suggested that they go for brunch to put into place the next part of her plan.

He took her to a nearby restaurant that served swanky food, the kind that dished up on plates made of some fossilized animal or other. Elise paled a little when she saw the prices, wondering how on earth she'd gloss that over with the expenses department, but Mark saw her expression and laughed.

"It's my treat." He told her generously after they had ordered. "You've changed my life for the better. Consider this my way of saying thank you."

"That's very kind but you may not feel so generous when I tell you what I have planned for today." Elise admitted and he immediately looked nervous.

"On a scale of one to ten how much am I going to hate it?" He asked tentatively and she grinned.

"That depends entirely on you." She fished around in her bag and produced an elastic band. "Please put this on your wrist." She handed it across the table to him and he stared at her like she had completely lost the plot. "Go on." She urged so he put it over his hand. "Good. Now, you and I are going to have a pleasant conversation like we are on a date and meeting for the first time and every time you say something negative about yourself I get to ping that elastic until you learn to stop putting yourself down all the time."

"You're kidding, right?" He was still staring at her like she'd gone nuts and she burst out laughing.

"No, I'm not kidding." Turning serious, she took his hand and looked him straight in the eye. "When we first met you spent the whole of our first conversation basically telling me you hated your job, you hated internet dating and you were a worthless human being. I've spent the last couple of days proving to you that you're not worthless and that you have very special gifts. Now I need you to learn to behave like a person of worth. It doesn't matter how special you are; if you keep putting yourself down all the time women aren't going to want to spend time with you."

To her astonishment his eyes filled with tears. "You're right." He took his hand back and wiped his face. "I guess I didn't feel like I had anything to be thankful for."

"And now?" Asked Elise gently, a little surprised at the intensity of his reaction.

"I'm not a worthless human being." He said quietly after a moment's pause. "If it had just been you telling me my pictures were great I might not have believed you, but Mark genuinely believes they're good as well. You could see it in his eyes. I have a gift."

"Yes. You do." Well this was an unexpectedly successful breakthrough and Elise was terrified it was going to come crashing in any second now.

"I know I have a long way to go," he told her honestly. "I've always been negative and I've always taken the criticisms of others to heart. I think maybe it's time to address that."

"Well, what goes around comes around." Elise nodded firmly. "I've always believed that. If you attack life with negativity then that's what you get in response, but if you attack it with positivity you'll reap the rewards of that over time."

"I'd rather you didn't put this in your blog, but I'm going to get counselling." He declared abruptly and then his face sagged in on itself as though he was relieved he had admitted this. "I...there are things..."

Sensing he was about to reveal something massively personal, Elise reached across and covered his hand. "Mark, you don't have to tell me this if you don't want to."

"No I do." He scrubbed his face again. "It's just difficult. I've never really spoken to anyone about it before but I think I need to."

"Okay." Elise settled in for the long haul. "I'm listening."

Over the next two hours as they ate he told her a story that was both sad and mesmerising. His father had been an alcoholic when he was growing up and had regularly beaten him and his mother to a pulp. His mother had killed herself when Mark was 17 and he had left home to study accountancy in an effort to get away. His father had died, just before Mark took his finals, of liver cirrhosis and Mark hadn't been to see him in the hospital. With his self-confidence at an all time low he had fallen into the classic pattern of ending up in an abusive relationship that had lasted almost 6 years. He had finally left her, a broken man, after she had landed him in surgery with a well placed golf club to the nether regions. With no outside help he had slowly built up his career and in the process had become a bitter, lonely and defensive man.

"But I'm ready to get help." He told her quietly. "I don't want to be this way anymore. You showed me that I need to be able to trust people because otherwise I'm going to totally self-destruct without ever actually living my life." His eyes welled up again. "I don't want to become my father."

"You won't." Elise told him fiercely. "Admitting you need help is the first step towards fixing this and I know you can do it. I *believe* you can do it. Can I help? Do you want me to look into counsellors for you?"

"No it's okay." He smiled tremulously. "I looked online after I left my ex and there's a male equivalent to the women's refuge but I was never brave enough or feeling worthy enough to actually call. I was going to look up the number and call them after I get home from the studio this afternoon."

"Good. Well...if you want me to come with you I can." Elise offered. "Or you can call me afterwards if you don't want to be on your own. You don't have to go through this alone."

He looked as though he was about to say something and then the tears spilled over. "Excuse me." Abruptly he got up and left the table, heading for the men's room at the back of the restaurant. Elise watched him go with a heavy heart. When she had considered this whole venture she'd had no idea at all that it would end up being so emotional and she found herself wondering if she would have been brave enough to attempt it if she'd had even the slightest inkling of the journey it would take her on with Mark. She sighed. Probably not, but now that she was here she was going to stick with it, whichever way it led. She had set Mark's feet on a journey towards becoming whole and she would see it through with him, independent of the feature and the magazine. After a lifetime of being given up on and abused she was damned if she was going to abandon him too. He deserved more. The trust he had placed in her was humbling.

When he returned from the bathroom his eyes were a little red but dry and his shoulders were a little straighter.

"Are you okay?" She asked quietly and he nodded.

"I am. I feel..." he searched for the word and then he smiled. "I feel lighter. I had no idea how much better I feel just from having told someone. Thank you so much."

"Don't thank me – that's what friends are for." Elise smiled at him. "I'm glad it's helped. Today is the first day of the rest of your life."

"Yes." His smile was dazzling. "I suppose it is."

When they got up to leave he paid the bill and then they stood in the sunshine outside. They were going in opposite directions and as far as the feature was concerned they wouldn't be seeing each other again. She would spend the following day writing up her blog and magazine article and he would be spending the morning re-drafting his dating profile for her to approve. Neither had any doubt they would see each other again but it would be as friends and not as partakers in a feature.

Impulsively he reached out and hugged her and she held him tightly for a few moments, trying to silently pass him strength. "Keep in touch okay?" She told him. "I'm not talking about emailing me your profile. I want to know how you get on with the counselling and if you have dates. I want to know how the photography goes. You've got my number. You can call me any time."

"I will." Shyly he plucked at the elastic band still encircling his wrist. "Can I keep this?" He asked and she grinned.

"Of course you can." She burst out laughing. "Who knew an elastic band could be so life changing?"

"I'll never look at one in the same way again." He agreed, plucking at it again in a way she just knew was going to become a habit. "I suspect I'll wear this one until it wears out."

"I have a box on my desk so let me know when it does and I'll send you another one." She joked. "You'd better go or you'll be late."

He checked his watch. "Yes, you're right. Thank you again. It's been an incredible experience."

"No, thank *you*." She hugged him again. "Be well Mark. Be happy."

"You too."

As she watched him walk away down the street it seemed to her as though he grew in stature with every step. Four days ago he had been a small and lonely man. Now he was probably the finest photographer she had ever met and had a friend prepared to help slay his personal demons. It was a good result and she felt both proud and humbled to be a part of it.

So here we are at the end of week one. To describe it as epic would be like comparing a hurricane to a fart. It's been life changing for both of us and, while that sounds grossly melodramatic, I'm prepared to stake my health and well-being on it not being an overstatement of the situation.

The idea of getting a photographer to appraise Mark's work was a good one. Said photographer was incredibly impressed. So impressed, in fact, that he has offered him an association with his studio and together they will be pitching to galleries to exhibit and sell Mark's work. I'm so proud of him I feel like I could burst. A few days ago he felt he had nothing of worth to write about himself and now, for the first time in his life, he's realising that actually there is a lot about him that's worth writing about.

He sent me his new profile to read this morning. It tells the story of a man who is passionate about photography. He explains how he sees the world in a way that allows him to take these incredible pictures and has added some of his work to the bottom to illustrate it. I defy any woman to look at them and not fall slightly for the man behind the lens.

He further tells the story of a man that loves to travel. So many of his photos are taken in third world countries where he has travelled extensively on a shoe string, totally immersing himself in the culture. Beneath his plain words about the places he has been and the people he has met runs an undercurrent of humbleness and affection that's both endearing and inspiring. I learned this morning that he actually speaks four languages fluently and enough pidgin in 6 or 7 others to get by. As a travel companion, I suspect he would be second to none. Underneath his gruff city exterior is a proper old-fashioned adventurer and if he was an archaeologist instead of a banker he would be probably be Indiana Jones.

It was like a master-class in profile writing. Funny, quirky and warm. If he doesn't get a date on the back of it I will eat my hat. Or at least I would if I had a hat. Failing a hat I will substitute cake. Actually no I won't. I like cake. I don't want to want him to fail. Perhaps I should say shoe...yes. If he doesn't get a date off the back of this new improved profile I will eat any shoe of his choosing.

But all of this would be nothing without an improvement in his personal manner. I remember back to that first day we met when I was so convinced we were going to fail because he was so bitter and defensive... People, I have discovered a new potential weapon of mass destruction. On a scale of one to amazeballs it rates around the level of awesomesauce. It is both cheap and easily deployable by anyone with absolutely no training.

Ladies and Gentlemen, I give you...*drum roll*...the rubber band. (Awaits applause).

No seriously, I was channelling my inner sadist and was determined to break him of the habit of putting himself down all the time so I cornered him in a restaurant and put an elastic band around his wrist. I told him we were going to pretend we were on a date and that every time he said something negative about himself I was going to ping the elastic band.

He clearly thinks I'm more of a sadist than I do because, in the entire two and a half hours we talked, he did not say one negative thing about himself. Not one. He said things that were honest and humbling, things that were personal and occasionally painful. There were tears on both *our parts and I strongly suspect I now know more about him than any other person on earth.*

It is both humbling and frightening to be the receptacle for so much honesty but I feel both honour and friendship bound to bear it with warmth and best wishes.

So now to the important question, the question all women would want to know if they were evaluating Mark as a prospective partner...if Mark was a cake, what would he be?

Chocolate fondant. Simples.

At 6pm she got an email from Taylor.

Dearest Elise, Your blog post has been approved. It made all of us in the editorial office laugh. You are a natural. I tried to get someone to explain the cake thing to me but it seems it is a 'woman thing' so I am going to assume it is a positive. I had to Google what a chocolate fondant was. I didn't know there was such a thing as a cake with a liquid centre. I am curious to try one sometime...

I thought you may like to know what Mark said about you. I have copied it below as it will appear in the magazine feature at the end of the month.
Taylor xx

"Meeting Elise has been one of the most profound and life-changing experiences of my life. I had thought I was meeting her to fix my issue with dating but it turned out that it wasn't my terrible dating technique that needed fixing at all. It was me. Until I could learn to accept myself, I was never going to accept what anyone else thought of me and you can't base a relationship, or even an attempted

relationship, on a situation where one side doesn't trust the other's opinion. It felt like she walked into my darkness armed with nothing but an elastic band and turned all the lights on. When we last met she told me that it was to be the first day of the rest of my life and I can't even begin to tell you how true that is. It has been a remarkable experience and I am a changed man. As for the dating? Well, watch this space..."

Elise felt a little tearful all over again reading Mark's words but when she returned to Taylor's her frown reappeared. Again with the kisses...and two of them this time. He'd also gone from no greeting to 'Dear Elise' and now to 'Dearest Elise'. It was strange. Perhaps he did want them to be friends again. Elise wasn't the kind of woman to hold a grudge and she wanted to just wipe the slate clean and forgive him but after their meeting outside the offices she wondered if she would ever be able to trust him not to turn again. She liked to invest in her friendships. It would be awful to assume someone was close to you only for them to suddenly go cold and distant.

She also found the whole open ended cake sentence a little odd. She wondered if this was a manly way of suggesting they go out for cake to iron out whatever differences he thought they had without actually asking her to go for cake. That would be such a guy thing to do. But given that all the wrongdoing seemed to have come from his side, it didn't make any sense that he would expect her to be the one to go out on a limb. She hadn't done anything to make him become distant other than refuse to sleep with him and she thought they'd had that all ironed out.

She read his words again and again before finally sighing. It wasn't in her to not give him a second chance, not when he was trying to be friendly. She typed a quick response about fondant definitely being a good thing, thanked him for passing on Mark's words and very carefully said nothing about going out for cake. She signed it off with a kiss, just one, and felt strangely relieved as it vanished from her outbox. It was horrible to think that she was in somebody's bad books without knowing why. Hopefully this would all sort itself out and they could be friends.

She cooked pasta for dinner and was about to settle in to watch a film afterwards when the buzzer for her door went. She frowned, looking at her watch. It was almost 9pm and she wasn't expecting any visitors.

"Hello?" She said into the phone, wondering if someone had pressed the wrong doorbell.

"It's Nathan."

"Oh hi!" She grinned. "Come on up!" Pressing the button to release the door she went to wait for him at the door to the flat. "I wasn't expecting you tonight!" She leaned up to give him a kiss on the cheek. "I was just about to watch a film. Come on in. Do you want a drink?"

"No thanks." He let her take his coat in silence and Elise realised something was wrong.

"What's up?" She asked as he followed her through to the living room. "You seem a little quiet."

"Who is he?" He asked and Elise blinked.

"Who is who?"

"Mr X."

Utterly bewildered Elise stared at him. "Mr who?"

He stared back at her and then his jaw dropped. "Do you not read the comments written on your blog?" He asked and she shook her head, blushing.

"No. I figured I might find it hard to take if anyone was mean."

He considered her for a long moment and then he started laughing. "You're so cute sometimes it's ridiculous. So you haven't seen the Mr X comments?"

"No. What are you talking about?"

"Get your blog up on the net and I'll show you." He made them both hot chocolate while she booted up her laptop and found her blog on the website. She hadn't even looked at it yet so she was astonished to see that her first post had already reached more than a thousand comments. Her third one which had only been up for a couple of hours was already into the three hundreds. It seemed the magazine was going all out to promote traffic to the site and it was working.

"This is crazy!" She felt like she was going a little boggle-eyed and her hand shook as she accepted a mug from him. "Did you read all of these comments?"

"No." He grinned. "I stopped about a third of the way down the fifth page. But they're all good so far. Look here..." He clicked on the link to her first post and went to the comments. Six or seven down, he pointed at a response. "Behold, Mr X."

Elise leaned in to read the comment.

"Für Elise...when I lie awake in the twilight hush it is the haunting melody of your namesake tune that flows through my thoughts. To me you are precious. Any man who is able to put his arms around you would not know how lucky he is. Even those of us that have held you in friendship are blessed. Ever yours..."

"Wow...that's kind of creepy." She stared at the screen. "What is he? A stalker?"

"I have no idea but either he has hugged you at some point or he thinks he has." Nathan pressed back on the browser and clicked on the link to her second post. "There he is." The comment from Mr X was about halfway down the first page of comments.

"Elise...it is an extraordinary gift to see such beauty in those around you and it seems to me that you don't know how extraordinary you are to be able to see the gifts in others. Each of those beautiful things you wrote about Mark could just as easily have been about you. There is a sweet innocence to your smile that touches everyone around you deeply. It focuses on a person and makes them feel like you

can see all the brightest and best parts of their soul. You make us better just by being around. Ever yours..."

"I don't know whether he's completely delusional or he really is someone I know." Elise didn't know whether to be flattered or freaked out. "This is exactly why I don't read these comments. I'm feeling kind of uncomfortable right now."

"Say for argument's sake it is someone you know," Nathan was taking her to the third blog post "how many guys do you know that have hugged you and would have known that you were blogging for the magazine?"

"It could be anyone." Elise shrugged. "It's been pretty well advertised for the last two months that features were coming and I would be one of the guest bloggers. Half the people in this country buy the magazine and the other half have probably flicked through a copy at some stage. It could be anyone I went to school with, anyone I've ever worked with...think about it Nathan. It could apply to you. It could apply to Harry. I hugged him the other night. It could apply to my boss. It could apply to Mark. I was always hugging guys at uni...some of my oldest friends are male. But apart from you I don't think that any of them find me attractive in that way."

"Well then we need to keep an eye on them. Eventually he'll mention something that will pinpoint who he is." Nathan stepped back and gestured for her to read the third comment.

"Elise...if you were a cake you would be a Christmas cupcake – small but perfectly formed with delicate white icing and decorations that evoke memories of that time of year when everything is brighter and joyful and reminds you of home and time in front of the fire learning what is most important in this life. You'd have a hint of cinnamon and vanilla...sweet and spicy. You will never come in batches of

twelve though. You are unique and there will never be another like you. Ever yours..."

"A Christmas cupcake?" Elise didn't know whether to laugh or be offended. "Really? A *cupcake*?!"

"Well what kind of cake did you think you would be?" Nathan seemed amused by her outrage.

"Something weird but satisfying like a chocolate and beetroot cake." She sounded so disgruntled that Nathan couldn't help himself. He burst out laughing even as he realised what she'd said.

"Chocolate and beetroot?" He screwed his face up. "That sounds gross."

"It's actually delicious." She told him primly. "In fact we'll bake one tomorrow. Unless you had plans?"

"Nope. And now that I'm here I'm kind of hoping you'd let me persuade you to give me somewhere to sleep so I don't have to go home."

Elise looked at him sternly. "So you came over uninvited, demanded to know who my secret admirer is, creeped me out with said secret admirer and then told me that the cake I perceive myself as sounds gross and *that* is your method of persuading me to let you stay over?" She got through it with a straight face...almost.

"Wow, when you put it like that I have been a little socially inept haven't I?" He looked sheepish. "I'm sorry. Can we start again? I missed you yesterday."

"I missed you too." Laughing she let him pull her up into a hug and they held each other close for a while. "Seriously though, should I be worried about this?" She asked and he sighed.

"I don't think so. It all seems fairly benign. We'll watch and see what happens." He rubbed her back soothingly. "I have a friend that works for the Police. If it looks like it's getting a little out of hand I'll call him and he can give you some advice."

"I'm sure the magazine has lawyers and stuff." Elise added, more to make herself feel better than anything else. "We'll be fine. It'll be ok."

"Totally."

It turned out that chocolate and beetroot cake was Nathan's new favourite and they made double so that they could take one to his mother's in lieu of flowers. They made cream cheese frosting for it which freaked Nathan out even more than the beetroot had until he actually tried it. Then he insisted on dyeing it pink to remain in keeping with the theme.

"I had no idea baking was so much fun!" He enthused as they walked towards the tube station. "We should do this more often."

"What do you mean more often?" Elise was amused. "We only met ten days ago. Surely you don't think we need to bake more than once a week?"

He actually considered it. "I guess I might get kind of huge." He admitted. "But it's tempting. Baking three times a week? Honey that's some kinda heaven."

"Three times a week?" Elise burst out laughing. "That's a recipe for whaledom. Once a week is my highest offer."

"If that's all you'll give me, I'll take it." Nathan grinned and bumped her shoulder affectionately.

"Hey, watch that cake box!" She steadied it and he flushed.

"Sorry. Little over-excited about the baking opportunities." Laughing, they headed into the station and away to meet his family.

"I can't believe you did that." Elise grumbled as they arrived back at his after dinner. They had turned up at his parent's to discover that his grandparents and two of his aunts were also there along with Harry. When she had looked at him, slightly panicked by all the people, he had looked sheepish. He'd known all along it was a family gathering. He thought that if he told her that she might have refused to go. She was honest enough to admit that he would have been right. As lovely as all his family members were, and they were really nice, they did give Nathan and Elise an extensive grilling. She had practically given them her entire life story by the time they got to the main course. Luckily she thought she had passed everything they threw at her with flying colours. She knew because Harry had high-fived her on the way out and his mother had hugged her warmly.

"But we had fun, didn't we? You were great!" Nathan gave her his most endearing smile and she relented slightly.

"They're going to hate me when I break your heart." She said morosely and he took her into his arms.

"Then don't break my heart." He replied simply as though that would fix everything.

"I'm only here for 3 months." She reminded him. "After that my contract runs out and I'll be away back to Scotland."

"A lot can happen in 3 months." He shrugged expansively. "There's no point borrowing trouble. We'll see what happens when we get there."

"I guess." She envied his easygoing manner. The three months was already looming large in her life. She didn't want to fall for Nathan only to have to leave him. That would be too cruel.

They spent another quiet weekend together. Elise didn't even turn her computer on. The realisation that their time was, for the moment, finite made her realise that she couldn't afford to waste a second of it.

Come Monday morning she kissed Nathan goodbye at the door and settled down to reacquaint herself with project two.

Chapter 6

I'm considering last week a success, whether Mark gets a date or not. As a result I'm slightly worried that I'm approaching this week with a wildly cavalier attitude, confident in a success that may have been a one off. After all, how many regular Joes (or in this case Daves) turn out to be a world class photographer? I firmly believe that everyone has at least one remarkable feature, one thing that makes them in some way special. It's just a question of finding that one thing and figuring out how to use it to make him desirable to women. Let's face it, if he's the world champion at gurning that's just not sexy. I might be a maestro with words but I'm not THAT good.

So. Dave. His profile is a total yawn-fest. If it had a soundtrack it would be the elevator version of The Girl from Ipanema. Bing bing bing ba bing bing bing...you know you were singing along just then.

It's one of those "I'm a nice guy who likes watching films and taking long walks in the forest" profiles. So far so Hannibal Lector. It's not improved any by a truly awful photo. It's clearly taken with a webcam and appears to show the top left hand corner of his face in close up. It is an obviously accidental photo and yet he has seen fit to put it as his profile picture. I'm not seeing the logic here. I wonder how he snapped it accidentally while setting up to take a proper one and had some sort of convoluted thought process that led him to decide it was a great idea to use it to attract women. Honestly, a goldfish armed with a webcam and amphetamines could take a better picture. Through the goldfish bowl. With one of those little stone bridges in the way. I think an hour or so at a photography studio is going to feature in our week because getting him a decent photo might be all he needs to find a woman desperate enough to bypass the boring. Unless there's a reason for only showing quarter of his face. Perhaps he is disfigured in some way.

Here's the thing, if he is...it's nothing to hide or be ashamed of. We all have our flaws. I personally have MANY flaws and while I don't flaunt them in people's faces I am at least honest about them. You read so many horror stories of people that go on dates with people they've met on dating sites only to discover that the person is ten years older or six inches shorter than they claimed. It seems to me to be an eminently stupid thing to do. You're going to get found out. It's inevitable. Doing it is only going to make people distrust you and that's not a decent basis for a new relationship. I could meet up with a guy who turned out to be handsome, charming and funny but if he'd lied about his age, even by 2 to 5 years, I'd still walk away. You'd spend the rest of your time together wondering what else he fibbed about.

If a person cannot accept you for who and what you are then they are the one who is flawed, not you. Beauty is not a chiselled jaw or a perfect platinum bob, it's a state of being. When I meet someone for the first time it's not their face or their body that I look at, it's their eyes. A lot of people's are just average everyday eyes...average people just coasting through their average lives. Some are utterly soulless...people stuck in the despair of lives they hate. But some, those that are most precious to me, twinkle away as though lit by an inner fire of joy. It's a man's eyes that I connect with first and the rest is all secondary. I don't care about scars or marks...it's the windows to your soul that hold the keys to my heart. So show me yourself, warts and all, and let beauty be in the eye of the beholder.

Satisfied with the post, she saved and opened up her email account to send it in to the editors. Once that was done she clicked through her unread emails. There were a few that had arrived over the weekend from the magazine and one from Mark, but then she found one sent that afternoon that made her blood run cold.

From: Mr X (_X_Towers@hotmail.com_)
To: Elise Waterford
(_elise.waterford@monochrome.co.uk_)

Elise,
I wanted to congratulate you on your first week in the new job. The blog posts have been entertaining and I'm looking forward to what's in store for this week's project. I don't know if you've read my comments on your blog but if you have you'll know that I think you're a very special woman.
Ever yours,
X

She stared at it for a moment and then clicked reply.

From: Elise Waterford
(_elise.waterford@monochrome.co.uk_)
From: Mr X (_X_Towers@hotmail.com_)

Who are you and how did you get my email address?

She waited a few minutes, clearing out her deleted items folder as she wondered if he was online, and then her computer pinged with the sound of incoming mail.

From: Mr X (_X_Towers@hotmail.com_)
To: Elise Waterford
(_elise.waterford@monochrome.co.uk_)

Elise,
It wasn't difficult to figure out. The generic server is monochrome.co.uk (hence the website address) and most

*companies use a first_name dot last_name format. As for who I am...well I'm not brave enough to tell you that just yet. Think of me as a secret admirer. You know me, we're friends, and perhaps eventually you'll figure it out but until then I shall continue to leave you love letters. It's the bright point of my week. *cheeky wink**

Ever yours,
X

Well she supposed that made sense. It was a generic email address format. Realising she was playing with fire but too curious to stop she clicked the reply button again.

From: Elise Waterford
(elise.waterford@monochrome.co.uk)
From: Mr X (X_Towers@hotmail.com)

X,
Now I am intrigued. Please tell me who you are?
Elise

She waited for half an hour, messing about with the settings on her desktop and playing a game of solitaire, but there was no response and eventually she switched the machine off.

* * *

On Tuesday Elise had agreed to meet Dave for coffee. If it was anything like her meeting with Mark she knew they'd eventually end up at his house because it was the place she could learn the most about him but she needed him to be comfortable with her and so they met on neutral territory. There turned out to be nothing wrong with his face at all and when she asked him about the photograph he simply shrugged and said it had seemed like a good idea at the time. He'd thought that there were so many faces on the site, something a little different might stand out.

It was another bland conversation. At least he wasn't putting himself down all the time like Mark but she was driving the entire conversation and it was hard work. It was like Dave just had nothing to talk about. Every question was met with a shrug and answers of five syllables or less. They spent an awkward twenty minutes sitting in silence when Elise decided to let him take charge of the situation. Eventually she sighed.

"I can't figure out if you're just shy or if you really don't have anything to say." She told him bluntly. "You need to work with me here or this isn't going to work."

"I find you intimidating." He flushed red and stared at his coffee. "You're so bright and articulate. It's quite daunting."

This time it was Elise that was startled into silence. "I'm just a regular woman." She managed eventually. "I'm here to help you, Dave. There's absolutely nothing special about me. Just because I'm well spoken it doesn't make me any different to you."

"Are you kidding?" He gaped at her. "I have your book you know?"

"Really?" Elise blushed, both flattered and pleased. "That's awesome. You're the first person that's not family who I know has got it."

"Really?" He grinned. "Maybe you'll sign it for me..." He looked so hopeful she burst out laughing.

"Sure I will. Come on, let's bounce this joint." They stepped out into the street and took in a lungful of the humid London air. Totally out of the blue Elise got a pang of homesickness for her little Scottish cottage with its fresh air and clear views. Shaking it off, she looked a little wistfully at the sky and then returned her attention to Dave. "So where do you live, Dave?"

"Not far from here." He looked shy about inviting her into his home. "It's just a couple of streets away."

She followed him as they walked for less than five minutes and he stopped outside a modest townhouse. It was nowhere near as large as Mark's had been but then Elise hadn't been expecting it to be. London was a crazy expensive place to live. She stepped through the door and took a moment to absorb the atmosphere. There was nothing as striking as Mark's photographs had been and for a brief moment her heart sank but she sucked it up and followed him through to the living room. There had to be something here she could use.

As Dave went through to the kitchen to fetch a glass of juice for her Elise walked slowly along the mantelpiece and studied the photographs on the mantel and on the wall above it. They showed a warm and connected family. Dave's parents, nieces and nephews, a couple of brothers and a sister...they were a nice looking family unit. In the centre spot above the mantel was a large framed picture of the younger woman from the family photographs, the woman Elise assumed was Dave's sister. Beneath it was stuck a chart with mostly empty spaces but a few stars stuck to it with a running total in the thousands of pounds scrawled next to them.

"What's this?" Elise asked as Dave returned. "What are the stars for?"

Dave looked up at the picture and his eyes filled with tears.

I've always wanted to learn the Argentine Tango. As dances go it's so sexy and funky, so precise yet fluid. I'd quite like to learn ballroom dancing in general and the Viennese waltz would come a close second, but it's the tango that floats my boat. I keep thinking that one of these days I'll find a class or instructor and learn it just for the sake of learning it. One of these days...

How often does that sentence feature in your life? Think of your dreams and ask yourself when you're going to get around to achieving them and chances are you're putting them off for some rainy, undefined day in the future. I know I have many dreams...I want to get another book published. I want to have a family. I want to travel to China to see the Terracotta warriors and the Forbidden City. I have these dreams in my heart but whenever I think about my current situation I'm always too busy, too broke, too unheeding of the urgency of anything. Because I have all the time in the world, right?

Wrong.

Dave is a man on a journey. Last year he lost his sister suddenly to cancer. She was 34. A lesser man might have been bowed by grief, become a shadow of himself, lost himself in the loss. Not Dave. He took the most important lesson of all from it...that life is too short. If you keep putting off your dreams for 'one day' it will be too late. You could get hit by a bus tomorrow, you could be in a car crash...or you could die of cancer at 34 with only two weeks' notice. You never know what is right around the corner. If you keep putting off your dreams then one day it will be too late to live them.

In honour of his sister, so that her death was not for nothing, Dave has created his bucket list. Refusing to leave his dreams for 'one day' he is ticking them off one by one and actually living them, day by day, week by week. He is working two jobs to pay for his list, but he's getting sponsorship for his achievements and donating it to cancer charities. It is an endeavour both brave and selfless. I am in awe of his determination to live life to its fullest. There has been so much sadness in his life, but he has been a beacon of light shining through it. If Dave was in charge of the world, no-one would ever die without fulfilling their dreams.

Unless those dreams involved world domination and bat-winged kittens of course. That would just be plain wrong.

He has already done the sky dive and bungee jump, he's done a six week tour of the Polynesian Islands, he's climbed to Machu Picchu and walked large sections of the great wall of China...all in one year. It's been a titanic effort, but he's not done. There are another fifteen items on his bucket list, but it is his last that I want to help him with.

Dave wants to leave behind a son, whether he dies this year or in a hundred years. That's why he started internet dating – to find a woman to marry, to live life to the fullest with and to create a legacy with. He just didn't know how to express that. He doesn't know how to speak of his emotions and that is a massive burden to place on anyone at a first date. Hi, I'm Dave...fancy getting knocked up? I understand now why his profile was so boring – it's too massive and emotional to speak of to those you do not know. Too much of a hope for the future to risk it on an unknown.

The thing is, if he is too afraid to speak his heart then he has let himself down. It makes a mockery of all his other dreams. You cannot live your life selectively and still expect it to mean something, and I know his heart...if he does not do this, if he gives up without leaving a son, his guilt at what he thinks will be letting his sister down will be almost unimaginable. Somehow he needs to swallow his fear of admitting to women what it is he's looking for and go out there and get it.

The hardest part is already done – he has told me, someone he admires and is a little intimidated by. I respect him; I do not judge him. Others will respond the same. I have a plan up my sleeve to help him become fearless, but for tomorrow I'm taking him to meet Mark (Project 1) to get a decent photograph done. After that? Well, you'll just have to wait and see.

It was late Tuesday night by the time Elise finished writing the blog entry and she left it for the following morning to read through because she was so exhausted she could barely see straight. It didn't have to be in until the afternoon anyway so she was already ahead of the game. Nathan had stopped by after work to see how she'd gotten on with Dave and they'd had dinner together but he'd gone home. With nothing to do until lunch time the next day, she had a long soak in the bath and then crawled gratefully into bed without bothering to set her alarm.

On Wednesday she woke up around mid-morning and went to switch her computer on. She wasn't meeting Dave until one o'clock so she decided to check her blog post one last time before sending it in. To her surprise there was another email there from Mr X. It had been sent first thing and she briefly wondered who she knew that was a morning person.

To: Elise Waterford
(*elise.waterford@monochrome.co.uk*)
From: Mr X (*X_Towers@hotmail.com*)

Elise,
Just wondering how you got on yesterday. I know last week was a pretty emotional experience for you and wanted to let you know that I'm here if you need to talk to someone about it.
Ever yours,
X

She couldn't decide if that was creepy or sweet. Giving him the benefit of the doubt she decided to answer.

To: Mr X (X_Towers@hotmail.com)
From: Elise Waterford
(elise.waterford@monochrome.co.uk)

> *X,*
> *That's very kind of you but I think I'll be okay. It's going to be another emotional week this week, as you'll see when the blog goes up later this evening. I'm sure it will end positively though and that's what I'm keeping in mind.*
> *Elise*
> *P.S. Can't you even give me a clue who you are?*

To: Elise Waterford
(elise.waterford@monochrome.co.uk)
From: Mr X (X_Towers@hotmail.com)

> *Elise,*
> *That's good to know. The offer stands though. I am always here, your patient and most caring admirer ;)*
> *Ever yours,*
> *X*
> *P.S. Is there a cake that likes to be mysterious? If there is, I'm that cake.*

You had to admire his persistence. Snorting with amusement, she shut down the computer and went for a shower.

At one o'clock she took Dave to meet Mark who had kindly given up his lunch break to take some photographs of Dave for the site. He didn't have a studio close enough to take them to, but a lot of his art was urban so it wasn't long before they found a suitable stretch of wall for Dave to pose in front of. Within twenty minutes Mark had a decent selection of photographs to pick through and develop and he and Dave had swapped phone numbers to compare experiences.

"Thank you so much." Elise hugged him as he packed his camera away. "I really appreciate this."

"It's the least I could do." Mark grinned. "I have a date on Friday."

"Really?" Elise was overjoyed for him. "That's awesome news!"

"Yeah I thought so too." He ran a hand through his hair and Elise was amused to notice a flash of elastic band beneath his cuff. "She got in touch with me the first day I put my new profile up. I've remembered everything you said and I'm going to give it my best shot."

"Good for you!" Elise's smile was so broad she thought if it got any wider the top of her head might fall off. "Please let me know how it goes. Call me on Saturday. I'd so love to hear it's going well for you."

"I will." He blushed. "Can I ask you a favour?"

"Sure." She waited expectantly while he hesitated.

"I'd really like to photograph you." He blurted out. "Mark says I can use the studio a couple of evenings next week. I've got a couple of other people lined up to take pictures of but there is so much light in your eyes...I was hoping-"

"Of course I'll do it." She felt uneasy being photographed, but she was taking a leaf out of Dave's book. Life was too short not to create keepsakes of the here and now. "I have one condition though."

"Anything you want." He promised solemnly.

"I'd like a picture to keep for me."

"I was going to give you one anyway." He blushed. "Keep the favour in the bank for a rainy day."

"I will." She hugged him again. "You're a sweetie. Text me when and where and I'll be there."

"I will." He shook hands with Dave and set off to tote his camera back to the office.

"He's got a date already. You're really good at this." Dave said to her with a touch of awe in his voice and Elise had to resist the urge to polish her fingernails.

"I try. But take note...this means when I tell you to do something I expect you to do it."

"Yes ma'am!" He trailed after her down the street and Elise hid her smile. It was all turning out so much better than she had expected.

Chapter 7

That afternoon Elise and Dave went for coffee and she asked him about the challenges on his bucket list that he had yet to do and where he was at with them. The fundraising alone took up a massive chunk of his time, never mind the effort to raise the money to do each item. His organisational skills were immense and he carted around diaries and notebooks with schedules and notes for everything he was doing at the current time. His family were helping him where they could but it hadn't come easily to them. It had taken them a long time to reconcile what they saw as selfish celebrations with losing his sister. It had been a long journey to understanding that he was doing the things that she never would in honour of her. Now they were fully behind him. It was such a poignant effort and Elise wondered aloud what he would do afterwards, when everything on his bucket list was complete.

"Well then I'll go on raising money but I'll maybe set up a bucket list foundation." He shrugged. "It can be like Make a Wish but for adults...people who are seriously or terminally ill getting to carry out their biggest dreams."

"I think that's a beautiful idea." Elise agreed fervently. "If there's ever anything I can do, let me know."

"I will." He smiled at her, full of hope. "I will."

To: Elise Waterford
(elise.waterford@monochrome.co.uk)
From: Mr X (X_Towers@hotmail.com)

Elise,
You weren't wrong when you said it was another emotional week. I'd love to take you dancing sometime.

Ever yours,
X

To: Mr X (X_Towers@hotmail.com)
From: Elise Waterford
(elise.waterford@monochrome.co.uk)

X,
Did you think I was exaggerating? Oh X, did you just ask me out on a date? Because, you know, if that's the case you'd have to tell me who you are...
Elise

To: Elise Waterford
(elise.waterford@monochrome.co.uk)
From: Mr X (X_Towers@hotmail.com)

Elise,
I'm not sure if you were being sarcastic or offended. It's so hard to tell in print. Was I asking you out on a date...good question. If I was, would you say yes?
Ever yours,
X

To: Mr X (X_Towers@hotmail.com)
From: Elise Waterford
(elise.waterford@monochrome.co.uk)

X,
It was sarcastic. I'm pretty hard to offend. As for the date, probably not because I'm kind of involved with someone. Unless you are secretly Robert Downey Jr. That would mean a whole rethink of my personal situation. A WHOLE rethink. Are you Robert Downey Jr?
Elise

**To: Elise Waterford
(***elise.waterford@monochrome.co.uk***)
From: Mr X (***X_Towers@hotmail.com***)**

Elise,
You are so weird sometimes. I still think you're cute.
Ever yours,
X

To: Mr X (*X_Towers@hotmail.com***)
From: Elise Waterford
(***elise.waterford@monochrome.co.uk***)**

X,
*That wasn't a no... o_o *freaks out**
Elise

Elise and Dave had a late start Thursday morning and met over lunch to start re-drafting his profile. Without making too much of an issue of his reasons for creating the list or the emotions behind it, they wrote several paragraphs about where he was coming from and where he was going. There was mention of his fundraising and charity events and it clearly shone through the words that here was a good, kind and genuine man who was living life to the full and wanted someone to share it with. After three hours of intense brain storming and editing, they finally had something for him to post on the website.

"Is that it?" Dave asked her as they both approved the final draft. "Am I free to be let loose into the wild?"

"Not yet." Elise grinned. "I have one last thing planned for you tonight and then you'll be ready."

"What's that?" Dave asked dubiously and Elise grinned.

"Well I know you can talk to me about what's going on with you, but I need to know that you can speak to other women," she explained. "Having an excellent profile is all well and good, but you need to engage in conversation. So after we've had dinner, you and I are going speed dating. Well, you are going speed dating. I'm coming along to supervise."

"Speed dating?" He looked a little queasy. "I don't think I like the sound of that. What happens?"

"Well there are a lot of men and women in a room and it works on a rotation. You get a set amount of time to talk to each woman and then when the bell rings you have to move on to the next woman. You score each other as you go along. The idea is to exchange as much information as possible in the time allotted to you to establish whether there's any connection there. If there is then you tick that you'd like to see them again and if you have both ticked the same box your details get exchanged and you arrange your own date."

"It sounds really complicated." He grumbled dubiously. "Are you sure about this?"

"It's really very simple." She bumped his shoulder cheerfully. "You'll be fine."

The first four dates were a disaster. As predicted, Dave had been faced with unknown women and had immediately clammed up. As they came away for a break, Elise already had a drink waiting for him and they sat to discuss the problem.

"You've got to stop answering with the basics." Elise told him. "They're interested in you so you need to tell them about you. When they ask you what you do for a living what do you tell them?"

"That I work in an office in the day and sometimes in a bar at night." She waited for him to expand but he didn't and she sighed.

"And that there is the problem. You either ask them what they do for a living and express interest in it or you tell them why you have two jobs. You should say that by day you work in an office and at night you work in a bar for the extra money because you're raising money for this, that and the next thing. You get what I'm saying?"

"Yes."

"Okay so if a girl asks you where you live, what do you say?"

"Bow Road."

Elise facepalmed. "No. You say 'I live in Bow Road. It's a nice area mostly and there's a great little shop around the corner from my house. Where do you live?' You've got to expand. Give her something to pick up on so the conversation doesn't fizzle out."

"Right." The bell rang to signal the next round and sheepishly he took his drink, promising to do better.

By the second break he was almost there and by the third break he was well and truly on the ball, keeping conversations going with every girl he sat with. Elise watched him proudly from the sidelines, trying to get sneak peeks of whether anyone wanted to see him again. It was a great moment to see him being so charming and chatty. He wasn't even tensing every time he approached a new seat any more, totally relaxed in himself now that he was in the zone.

As they walked back to the tube station afterwards he was laughing gleefully at the phone numbers clutched in his hand. The last five women he had spoken to all wanted to see him again and if he didn't get any bites from the internet dating he was going to call them. He was so excited it almost brought tears to Elise's eyes.

Nathan was waiting for her at the tube station where she was dropping Dave off because he hadn't been happy about her travelling home alone so late at night. He shook Dave's hand and then took Elise's as they waved the elated project two away on a train.

"You look tired." Nathan told her, tucking a loose strand of hair behind her ear. "Was it hard work?"

"Unbelievably." She tried not to yawn but she couldn't help it. "He's on the right path though. He'll find the right woman and sooner rather than later. He's a good guy."

"I know. I read your blog." They stepped onto a train heading in the direction of the Wharf and sat down in the almost deserted carriage. "I can't imagine what that must have been like." He continued as they watched London fly by in a blur. "I tried to think what it would be like to lose Harry and my mind just couldn't comprehend it. It was too much."

"I know." Elise agreed quietly. "I don't know what kind of strength of character it must have taken to not be crushed by it...to actually become a better person because of it. It's extraordinary."

"I think we'll all learn lessons from this week." Nathan told her. "I got you something." He rummaged in his pockets until he eventually found an envelope. It was a little battered but it clearly hadn't been in his pocket for very long.

"What are you buying me presents for?" Elise laughed as she opened the envelope. "I haven't done anything special."

"I disagree." His eyes twinkled as they flashed past another station. "You do something special every day just by existing. But this is different. This is taking a leaf out of Dave's book. I might lose you in ten weeks time so we need to cram in as many of the dreams from our collective bucket list as we can."

She knew what it would be before she even pulled out the vouchers entitling her to dance classes. "Oh my God!" She squealed excitedly. "It says these are for two! Are you coming?"

"Of course I'm coming." He laughed as she hugged him. "I looked up the Argentine Tango on Youtube. It's pretty sexy. I'm thinking I'd quite like to see that. Apparently this guy specialises in it."

"Oh my God!" Abruptly her eyes filled with tears. "Thank you so much!" She struggled to stop them from falling and he hugged her again. "These must have cost you a fortune."

"Not really. And it was totally worth it for the look on your face right now. Money is just money...you can't take it with you when you go."

That was true. Life was for living and that was exactly what she intended to do.

Nathan stayed over at hers and made her breakfast before he headed off to work the next morning. Elise was feeling lazy after her late night so after her morning shower she dressed in a tracksuit and sat down to write her final blog post of the week.

I once read that the secret to hosting the best parties is to learn something interesting about each of your guests and use it as an introductory ice-breaker. Hi so-and-so, this is such-and-such the accountant. Such-and-such, this is so-and-so. He's into snow-boarding too... This gives your guests a point of origin from which to start a conversation and you can then leave them to it and flow on to the next introduction. Of course, if you are wicked like me you'll make up facts just for the amusement value. Huckleberry, this is Doodlebug and he breeds giraffes. Doodlebug this is Huckleberry and he's a drag queen in his free time. It still has the intended effect – they have to talk to each other to sort out the facts from the fiction – it's just a lot funnier when you see their eyes widen.

I think this is an important lesson for my projects. For one reason or another both Mark and Dave have been painfully inept at conversing with a woman. Having a decent profile will help of course, because it puts their interesting facts out there for the conversation to be struck from, but unless they can expand on that conversation it's going to go nowhere. Dave had issues with this and as his hostess for the week it was important for me to teach him this valuable art. There's only one place I know you can go where you can have multiple attempts at conversations with total strangers in one place. I took him speed dating.

It was like watching the verbal equivalent of a gazelle on ice. He was a man of sprawling monosyllabic answers and very little else. How anyone can run out of things to say in less than five minutes is beyond me. A conversation about the weather can take longer than five minutes and I know that this is a man who has a lot in his life to discuss. On listening carefully I discovered that he doesn't link things in his head. If someone asked him his job he'd tell them what his jobs are and that's it. It didn't occur to him to explain why he was doing two jobs which would have led into a whole other section of conversation. It was painful.

I had to give him two pep talks (and 3 secret vodkas in his lager) before he finally got the hang of it. And he was good at it. By the end of the night, his natural charm and honest heart had won him no less than five phone numbers. It was an all round excellent result.

We've worked on his profile and it's ready to go up on the dating site tonight. I introduced him to Mark (project one) who took some great pictures of him for his profile. I'm pretty confident he'll be successful in finding dates. He's an average looking guy with an attitude towards life that one can't help but love. I suspect that when he does find The One it will be a wild ride for them...a lifetime of seizing each and every day by the balls and wringing out every last drop of joy.

All in all it was a week just as epic as last week. I have learned important things about life and I would be a coward not to put them into practice. Life is too short not to live it to the max and love every moment. You never know what is right around the next corner. For him I hope it's a good (fertile) woman but for me...well, I'm going to learn that tango.

The question of the week – if Dave was a cake what would he be?

Carrot cake with a sweet chilli frosting.

As she was going through to correct typos and grammatical errors, the tone on her inbox pinged and some weird sixth sense told her it was Mr X before she maximised the window to look.

To: Elise Waterford
(elise.waterford@monochrome.co.uk**)**
From: Mr X (X_Towers@hotmail.com**)**

Elise,
This Dave sounds like a wonderful guy. I really hope you can help him find someone. I can't imagine experiencing that sort of loss and I'm glad he's got you to help him achieve the things he doesn't know how to achieve on his own. It's made me think a lot about my bucket list. I think I'll start one this evening, all those things I want to try before it's too late. Does Dave have a website or a just giving page? I'd really like to help him out, make a donation.
Ever yours,
X

Not knowing his identity was frustrating but Elise couldn't deny that he actually seemed like a caring kind of guy and she fired off a quick email to him in response.

To: Mr X (X_Towers@hotmail.com**)**

X,

If you look at my feature page on the website there's a link to his just giving page on there. I'm sorry, I can't remember it off the top of my head. Thank you for donating. It will mean a lot to him that strangers are helping him out. Guess we all have a bucket list :)

Elise

Nathan came round straight after work and they cooked dinner together again. He watched as she pan-fried salmon fillets and whisked up lemon vinaigrette for the potatoes with something akin to awe on his face. He was clearly a microwave meal man when he was on his own and proper home-cooked food was still a novelty to him. They sat at the table and were chattering cheerfully away when they heard Elise's computer beep from the study.

"What was that?" He looked around and Elise grinned awkwardly.

"Just an email. It's probably Taylor telling me my blog post is online. If they wanted me to edit it I would have heard already."

"Oh right." He played with his food for a moment. "Have you read what Mr X has to say this week?"

"Nope." She replied cheerfully, chowing down on a huge forkful of fish.

"He's still posting after very blog." It was still clearly irritating him if his sudden moodiness was anything to go by and Elise set her knife and fork down.

"Nathan the fact that I haven't read it should tell you unequivocally that I really don't care. I don't care who he is or what he's writing. As far as I'm concerned you're the only man in my life right now and you're the only man I *want* in my life. Whoever this Mr X is can write whatever he wants. I'm just going to ignore him until he gets the picture and goes away." That wasn't entirely true because she was desperately curious to know who he was, but so far his emails had been entirely non-inflammatory.

"But aren't you even just a tiny bit curious?" He persisted. "If it is someone that knows you wouldn't you rather know who it is?"

"Not particularly." She replied calmly. "Knowing won't change anything other than possibly costing me a friendship. If you want me to then I'll go and read them but it won't change anything. I'm still yours."

"Okay. Fair enough. I can understand why you aren't bothered but it's a little weird that he's posting this stuff. You should keep an eye on it at the very least in case he does turn into some weird stalker."

"Okay, I'll check it. But don't worry about it." She smiled at him reassuringly and they continued dinner.

Afterwards he went to run them a bath while Elise checked her emails. Sure enough the blog had been approved and she had a short email from Taylor but she didn't bother drafting a reply to it. There was nothing urgent and he hadn't progressed past the two kisses so their tentative friendship was still on track. She was sure he wouldn't mind waiting for a response, especially given that it was Friday night.

Mindful of her conversation with Nathan, she brought up the internet and went to the blog to read Mr X's comments.

Monday – *Elise, I cannot believe that you are flawed. To me you will always be perfect. Each little thing that you consider a flaw just makes you more interesting, makes you more perfect. If beauty is a state of being then you will walk in it all the days of your life...your heart is too big to allow for any less. Ever yours...*

Wednesday – *Elise, I envy the ability to live for the day...to follow my dreams. The truth is that my dreams involve you but I am too scared to tell you to your face that I love you. I cannot embrace my own mortality enough to overcome my fears, but know that I will love you in silence until perhaps 'one of these days' I will be brave enough to speak my feelings to you out loud. Ever yours...*

Friday – Elise, As I read the end of this post I didn't think I could put it any more eloquently than the song...from my heart to yours: [Youtube_Ronan Keating_I Hope You Dance]

Elise, I hope you dance. Ever yours...

"Damn it!" She muttered as she closed down the browser. That was one of her all time favourite songs and now she was going to have it in her head for the rest of the night.

"Bath is ready!" Nathan called through and Elise sighed, scrubbing her face with her hands to shake off the uncomfortable feeling the comments had left in her. Maybe she would sing that song for Nathan, associate it with him in her thoughts and not this nameless, faceless stranger. He would understand, she was sure. She wished she had never read the comments.

"What did he write tonight?" Nathan asked, judging her tense moodiness correctly as they settled in the bubbles together.

"Not much. He quoted me a song." She sighed and tried to relax into him. "It just irritates me because I love that song and I don't want to think of him when I sing it. I don't want to associate it with frustration."

"I'm sure I can help you with that." His hand traced a lazy arc across her collarbone. "Do you think he quoted it because he knows you like it or was it just coincidence?"

"Coincidence I think." Elise frowned as she thought about it. "It seemed appropriate to the post."

"Ah well. Forget about him. Hey, we've got our first dance class tomorrow." He tugged her hair playfully and she grinned.

"Before or after baking?"

He gasped. "I'd forgotten tomorrow was baking day!" He twined her hair thoughtfully around his fingers. "Well class is at 3pm so I guess we can bake in the morning. I really want to bake."

"You're so cute." She laughed. "Okay, we'll bake in the morning. I got ingredients while I was at the shop today. I thought we'd make muffins."

"Sounds awesome. What flavour muffins?"

"Raspberry and almond. I have a really nice recipe and they're quite simple to make."

"They sound lush." He sighed happily. "I don't know how I ever lived without you. If you're not careful I might ask you to marry me one of these days."

Elise burst out laughing. "After two weeks? Are you nuts?"

"Two and a half weeks." He corrected. "And don't you think what we've got is special?"

She thought about how they'd slotted so seamlessly into each other's lives, how they laughed almost non-stop, how she felt about him... "Yeah I do." She said quietly. "But we're still in the honeymoon period. Two weeks isn't long enough to base the rest of our lives on."

"Two and a half. I know that. I'm just kidding really." His arms slipped around her and he held her close. "Would it scare you if I told you that I love you?"

"No." She swallowed thickly. "I feel the same. I just don't know how it happened so quickly."

"There was cake involved." He joked, half-seriously. "That always helps."

"Yeah, there was me thinking that it was the windows to your soul that hold the key to my heart but really it's the cakes in my stomach..." Elise burst out laughing, threatening to slosh water over the side of the tub.

"I didn't say it was the whole reason!" He protested, laughing with her. "Just that it helped."

"Whatever Nate, whatever..."

They slept in late, although Elise was woken up by a call from Mark about his date (went well but no sparks flew so they were both going to continue looking), but still managed to get a couple of batches of muffins made before lunch. Nathan had demolished four before she reminded him about their dance class and he decided to balance it out with only a small helping of the Greek salad and fresh bread she made for lunch. She was still laughing at him grumbling about his tummy as they got on the train to head into the city for the dance class.

They arrived at the studio well ahead of time and sat in a small gallery overlooking the dance studio while they waited their turn. Elise couldn't believe how nervous she felt watching all the dancers whirling below her. They seemed so graceful and in sync with each other that she didn't think she'd ever be able to move like that. It was a daunting prospect.

When their turn finally came they headed down into the studio to meet their instructor. He was a short Hispanic man called Luis who more than made up for his lack of height with boundless enthusiasm. But after putting them through some stretches he worked them hard, drilling them again and again on their posture and their walk. It was so much to remember all at once and it wasn't until they were into their second hour that Elise finally felt she was getting it. Trying to get the fluid slide while maintaining her posture and keeping her shoulders down at the same time as not falling over Nathan was difficult but she loved every moment of it.

"You both have a natural rhythm." Luis congratulated them as they cooled down after the session. "I think dancing will suit you. Do you wish to continue with the lessons?"

Nathan looked to Elise to say it was her decision and she grinned broadly. "We'd love to. When can you fit us in?"

He walked out to the reception area with them and flicked through his diary. "I have three slots a week free at the moment for one on one tuition." He perused through the pages. "They are all evenings unfortunately, but I have spaces available in my group classes. I would recommend you join at least one group class a week. This particular dance is a very social dance. It would do you good to see it danced in a social setting."

Eventually they settled on solo classes on a Tuesday and Saturday with a group class on a Thursday evening. Nathan would have to come straight from the library on the weekdays but he didn't mind that.

"Thank you so much!" Elise slid under his arm as they left the studio. "I enjoyed that so much! It's the best present anyone has ever given me."

"You're welcome." He hugged her and kissed the top of her head. "I'm surprised I enjoyed it as much as I did. Just don't expect me to get a fake tan. Or wear spandex."

"I won't." She couldn't resist poking a little fun. "I think you'd look pretty sexy in a three piece suit though."

"Oh really?" He drawled it out in an amused way. "Well, I tell you what...when we're good at this dance I'll wear the three piece suit out dancing one night if you wear a sexy little dress and flowers in your hair."

"Like a proper senorita?" She laughed. "Okay, I can do that. You got yourself a deal."

"Excellent."

They had a quiet night in, doing some dance practice and eating muffins in between films. Elise had been intending to freeze half of them but she didn't think she was going to get a chance the rate Nathan was inhaling them at. She wondered how on earth he stayed so slim.

On Sunday morning he made her breakfast in bed and then they went for a walk and a picnic in Hyde Park for a late lunch. Elise took her guitar and they sat in the sunshine eating their sandwiches while she strummed away and sang to him. It was a perfect afternoon crowned by an invitation to a barbecue at the Wimbledon house where their friends lived. They didn't even bother to go home, packing the remains of their sunny afternoon into the rucksack and getting on the underground straight there.

"I'm so stuffed!" Elise laughed as they arrived back at the apartment that night. "I feel like all we've done all day is eat!"

"That's because all we've done all day *is* eat." He laughed.

It was only nine o'clock when they got back as they both had to work the next day and Nathan was in the shower when the doorbell rang. Surprised, Elise picked up the phone wondering if someone had the wrong house.

"It's me, Taylor." Even through the intercom the rich timbre of his voice was unmistakeable.

Damn it. "Hi Taylor, come on up." She stuck her head through the bathroom door. "Nate my boss is here." She called through the steam. "Don't come wandering out naked or anything."

"Sure thing." He stuck a head full of soggy curls out the shower door and winked at her. He looked pretty damn fine all wet like that and Elise had to mentally give herself a shake before she threw caution to the wind and climbed in with him.

A knock on the door pulled her out of her daydream and she went to open it.

"Hi." She grinned at Taylor as she opened the door. "I wasn't expecting you this evening."

"Hi to you too." He leaned in and kissed her cheek. "I happened to be passing on my way home from an event and thought I'd stop in and see how you were settling in since it wasn't too late."

"I thought that was a rather spiffy suit." She grinned as she stepped back to look his full length. It was a beautiful suit tailored closely to show off the finest parts of his physique. There were a lot of spectacularly fine parts of his physique. "Would you like a coffee?"

"That would be lovely."

They were in the kitchen discussing the blog when Nathan appeared, his curls still wet but dressed casually in jeans and a sweater. Taylor obviously hadn't realised he was in the apartment and didn't look happy to see him there.

"Taylor this is Nathan. Nathan this is Taylor, my boss." Elise introduced, wincing inwardly as they clearly took a moment to size each other up.

"Nice to meet you." Nathan stuck his hand out and Taylor shook it. "I've heard a lot about you."

"I wish I could say the same." Taylor's tone was intended to be charming but it came across as slightly cutting. "Are you a friend of Elise's?"

Nathan slid a possessive arm around her. "I'm her boyfriend, yes."

"How wonderful." Taylor switched his gaze to Elise. "I had no idea you'd met someone."

"We haven't spoken much since I came down to London." She pointed out. "I met Nathan when I moved here."

"I see." His scrutiny was making her uncomfortable. "I actually came to ask you a favour. There's a charity ball next Friday night that's being hosted by the magazine. As our newest and brightest star I was hoping you would attend with me. There are several members of the editorial team that would like to meet you."

"I'd love to but I didn't pack anything suitable for wearing at a ball." Elise demurred, realising that the minute anyone said 'date' this was all going to go pear-shaped.

"I didn't think you would have so I spoke with the fashion department before I left work on Friday evening.

They're expecting you to stop by at the offices during the day on Friday and will outfit you with something suitable."

There was no way to refuse without coming across as churlish so she did the only graceful thing she could and accepted. She wanted to smack the brief smile of triumph he flashed at Nathan off his face but settled for visibly sliding her hand under Nathan's top instead to caress the tense muscles of his back. Taylor's jaw twitched and he swallowed the last of his coffee.

"Well it was lovely to meet you Nathan and good to see you Elise." He straightened up. "It's getting late so I'll leave you to it."

"Nice to meet you too." Nathan poured on so much charm it almost drowned out the sarcasm. Almost. Elise swatted him when Taylor turned round with a look that told him to be nice and followed Taylor to the door.

"Thanks for stopping by. It's been good to see you." She told him honestly. "Sorry I didn't reply to your last email – I've been out most of the last couple of days."

"That's okay. How is your wrist?" She held it up for him to see.

"All better now."

"Good." He gave her a lingering kiss on the cheek and then left in a flurry of expensive cologne and thousand pound suit.

"That man is so smooth I'm surprised his clothes don't just slide off him." Nathan declared grumpily and Elise burst out laughing.

"He's also split personality I think. When I first got down here he was so unbelievably rude I didn't know what to make of it and now suddenly he's Mr Nice Guy. Don't you worry, he'll go back to being rude in no time. I'm sure of it."

"I'm not." Nathan sighed. "There's nothing like a challenge to get a man's sex drive raging. Now that he knows you have a man he'll want you even more."

"He doesn't want me." Elise locked the door and headed for the bathroom. "He told me when we were in Scotland that he thinks of me just as a friend, that he doesn't find me attractive."

"He was lying." Nathan followed her and watched appreciatively as she stripped off to climb in the shower. "He wants you."

"He doesn't. But even if he did it's not going to happen." She waited for the water to warm up. "Mostly because I'm with you but even if I wasn't I wouldn't go there. I don't have relationships with people I work with, period. It doesn't work."

He sat on the edge of the bath while she wet her hair and soaped up. "Do you think he's Mr X?" He asked and Elise laughed.

"Taylor? No. He hasn't got a romantic bone in his body. I'm pretty sure he'd never listen to Ronan Keating either."

"He might not be romantic but he certainly knows how to be charming." Nathan pointed out sourly. "I think he'd do anything if he thought it would impress you."

"Well I'm not impressed." Elise rinsed out her hair and started again.

"You'll be careful on Friday won't you?" He asked after a short silence and Elise turned to look at him.

"You have nothing to be worried about." She told him quietly. "I told you I love you and I meant it. You need to trust me on this."

"I do." He was clearly struggling for words. "It's just...he has so much more than me."

"More what?" She stared at him. "More money? Bigger houses? You think that makes a difference to me?"

"No that's not what I meant." He looked upset as he tried to put it into words. "If he does like you maybe it's wrong of me to stand in the way. He could give you a better life than I ever could."

Stunned, Elise just gaped at him. "I can't believe you just said that."

"I don't mean it really, it's just a thought that's crossed my mind." He rubbed his hands through his hair. "I'm trying to explain why I trust you but I'm still worried about Friday."

She didn't like it but she could see where he was coming from. "You have nothing to worry about." She reiterated. "I don't want Taylor. I don't care how much money he comes with or how many houses. I don't want his accounts and I sure as hell don't want his disposable lifestyle. I'm a simple girl with simple likes and right now I'm liking me some sexy geek. Get your ass in this shower right now and help me scrub my back."

He smiled. "I love it when you talk dirty..."

Chapter 8

On Monday morning Elise sat at her computer and decided to write Mr X an email. His comments the week before had been on her mind all weekend and she still couldn't get that song out of her head.

To: Mr X (X_Towers@hotmail.com)
From: Elise Waterford
(elise.waterford@monochrome.co.uk)

X,
I'm going to come right out and say it – I think you're coming on a little strong here. You won't tell me who you are but you're quite happy to post online to hundreds of followers that you love me? And really? "Love"? Don't you think that's a little extreme? Also, I'm not perfect. No-one is. You need to take me down from whatever pedestal you've put me on and examine this situation objectively. You'll see that you're being entirely unreasonable.
Elise

Having said her piece, she closed down her inbox with a righteous clack of the mouse button and set to work on her next man.

I confess to being a little confused by this week's project. His name is Jim and, from first reading, his profile is actually all right. He's a 23 year old primary school music teacher who loves to cook and also has an interest in films. If I was trawling through a dating site and saw his profile I'd consider contacting him, especially since his picture is actually quite nice. He's blond with those almost elfin looks that Lord of the Rings made fashionable all those years ago. Come on ladies, you know who I'm talking about...you telling me you didn't have dreams about being rescued by a dashing dude in green who could pin you to a tree from a hundred paces with his bow and arrows so he could have his wicked way with you? No? Just me then...ahem.

Anyway, moving swiftly on, I can't understand why he hasn't been successful. Trawling through his file I came across a comment he had made that he has plenty of contacts but he speaks to girls once and then he never hears from them again. He seems just as bemused by this as I am. He's clearly a literate man. He has a teaching qualification and unless he got someone else to write the answers to his questionnaire he's obviously articulate. The only thing I can think is that he is so obnoxious to talk to that women won't give him a second chance.

This scares me.

It scares me because my gift is to bring out the best in people, show them the things in their life that they have cause to be thankful and joyful for. I like to give people a little faith in themselves. I can't change something fundamental about a person. It's like baking a perfectly balanced cake. If you have a plain sponge you can enhance the vanilla a little to make it richer and sweeter than it was, but if it's a chocolate cake then adding vanilla will do nothing because it's drowned out by the cocoa. If this man is truly obnoxious then finding the best things about him and enhancing them will be for nothing because women will still not want him.

I know the only way to find out is to meet him but I'm afraid that this week will be a challenge of an entirely different nature to the last two.

Her cursor hovered over the inbox icon. Something told her there would be an email back from Mr X but she really needed to send the blog post in. Cursing softly she opened it up and sent the blog before opening the email that had arrived, as expected.

To: Elise Waterford (*elise.waterford@monochrome.co.uk*)
From: Mr X (*X_Towers@hotmail.com*)

Elise,
I can't decide if you're mad at me for saying I love you or mad because, like me, you've probably been singing that damn song all weekend, which means I've been on your mind and that's bound to drive you up the wall when you don't know who I am. I wish I felt guilty about that but actually I'm kind of amused. I've been thinking about you too. Believe me, I've looked at the situation objectively. That's precisely why I can't tell you who I am. I desperately don't want to lose your friendship. You are a truly remarkable (and perfect!) woman. *Admires pedestal and polishes a speck of dust from the surface*
Ever yours,
X

She couldn't help herself from smiling at his cheek and ended up clicking reply.

To: Mr X (*X_Towers@hotmail.com*)
From: Elise Waterford (*elise.waterford@monochrome.co.uk*)

X,
I'm just mad at you full stop.
Elise

The reply was almost instantaneous.

To: Elise Waterford
(elise.waterford@monochrome.co.uk)
From: Mr X (X_Towers@hotmail.com)

Elise,
Anger, love...they're both just facets of passion. Score one to me?
Ever yours,
X

She hated to admit it but playful X was actually fun to correspond with and her fingers hovered over the keys as she wondered whether to reply or not. "Fuck it." She murmured softly and decided to play along.

To: Mr X (X_Towers@hotmail.com)
From: Elise Waterford
(elise.waterford@monochrome.co.uk)

X,
If we're keeping score I've knocked you out of the ball park. In your own words I am 'perfect', 'precious', 'extraordinary', 'unique', 'special' and 'interesting'. You on the other hand are, in your own words, too afraid to tell me who you are and afraid of your own mortality. Current tally is Elise 6: X minus 2.
Elise

To: Elise Waterford
(elise.waterford@monochrome.co.uk)
From: Mr X (X_Towers@hotmail.com)

Elise,
I think being a smartypants deducts at least one point from your score.
Ever yours,
X

To: Mr X (X_Towers@hotmail.com)
From: Elise Waterford
(elise.waterford@monochrome.co.uk)

> X,
> I disagree. It merely proves me right when I say I'm not perfect. Elise 7: X minus 2. Now I have work to do. Don't you have something more productive to do with your day? Oh yes, that's right, I don't know what you do with your day because you won't tell me. *sarcasm abounds*. Go do something productive with your day.
> Elise

To: Elise Waterford
(elise.waterford@monochrome.co.uk)
From: Mr X (X_Towers@hotmail.com)

> Elise,
> Yes ma'am! *Sings* I hope you dance...
> Ever yours,
> X

To: Mr X (X_Towers@hotmail.com)
From: Elise Waterford
(elise.waterford@monochrome.co.uk)

> X,
> You bastard. Elise 7: X minus 1.
> Elise

Elise met Jim early on Tuesday morning at the ice cream bar in Harrods. In person he looked just like his picture, tall and willowy with a hint of muscle in the arms, blond locks sticking out waywardly in a tousled mass on his head. If he'd just kept his mouth shut he would have been a perfect date.

After half an hour with him Elise could entirely understand why women never spoke to him more than once. It wasn't that he was a chauvinist, quite the opposite in fact, he was just so opinionated and crushing of everything that didn't agree with his world view that he unintentionally put her down several times. After having something she said utterly rubbished without any reasonable premise or explanation for at least the fifth time Elise could feel her temper flaring and decided to change the subject before she said something in anger and quit the whole project.

She asked how he got on with the kids at the school. Suddenly he changed and warmth seeped into his tone as he discussed the kids. He didn't particularly enjoy his job and very quickly his tone became unbearably pretentious as he discussed a musical he was composing for the school play but it had been there...a brief flash of warmth underneath the arrogance and bluster. It gave Elise pause for thought.

After another painful half hour she stopped him and asked for some names and details with a vague idea in mind of what she was going to do and left him in the shop to get busy.

It turns out I was right to be scared. Jim may be a handsome chap but in person he's as smooth as the offspring of a porcupine and a rusty cheese grater. After an hour in his company I couldn't bear to go back to his house as I had with the others and left him at the place we had coffee to come straight back to my computer to get to work.

He was utterly crushing. Everything I said that didn't agree with his beliefs was just dismissed or trashed without explanation or logic. I have never before met anyone as vocally narrow-minded as this man. It was weirdly childish in a way, like when a boy declares that girls are stupid with no real understanding of why or how he thinks that. There

*was no arguing with him because there was no logic there –
you couldn't debate the premise of anything because each
thought or idea was just cut dead in its tracks with
contempt. It was bizarre.*

*And then we moved on to the utterly ridiculous. In a
desperate attempt to find something he couldn't be rude
about I asked him about his job. There was a brief flash of
something human under his glacial exterior and then he
spouted the most outrageous tumbling of pretentious drivel
I have EVER heard. It seems he is writing a musical to be
performed by the kids at his school all about the 'emotional
response of special needs children to music of the 21st
century'. I just about snorted ice cream through my nose.
What man in his right mind would write a musical for a
bunch of 5 to 7 year olds on a topic like that? I can't even
begin to describe the mental images scrolling through my
head but I can tell you they involved toddlers in togas with
stick-on beards. Worse, can you imagine the total
bemusement of parents coming along to watch the school
play and being confronted with a group of such young kids
trying to portray such a concept? If it hadn't been so
earnest I'd have been laughing out loud, but as it was I left
feeling grumpy and irritated and in need of a hot stone
massage.*

*This week is going to be an epic challenge and,
strangely, possibly just as emotional as the last two. I say
this because of that tiny little flare of humanity that came
to life when he thought of the kids. Somewhere underneath
that glacial, rude and abrupt exterior is something warm
and alive and it needs to be brought out of its shell.*

*Many years ago I read somewhere that the persona
we present to people is not necessarily who we really are.
We all wear masks as a result of our upbringings and
childhoods. They're protection against the world we live in*

and not a true reflection of what lies beneath. The saddest thing is that most people don't realise that. There are few people I know that have been on a journey of self-discovery to understand themselves and even fewer who have truly faced what lies within. I personally have been through the counselling process and I can tell you honestly that it's a brutal process. To understand how you came to be who you are, you need to strip yourself right back to your basic components and look at how they were formed together to make you. You need to accept that you do have faults and that, in some instances, your own complacency allowed others to shape your personality in a way that's not for the better.

To understand who you are you need to understand how you came to be.

I believe that Jim has been through some things in his life that have forced him into a caricature of himself. I don't believe that anyone can be so glacial and arrogant without having been forced to be that way because of some great hurt or trauma in years past. I know that underneath his obnoxious exterior there is something warm and fuzzy dying to be nurtured. What I <u>don't</u> know is if I, personally, am strong enough to change him.

It's one of those awful situations where you have to be cruel to be kind and what I have in mind is going to hurt him. It's going to be a journey that takes him to the darkest places of his own mind and forces him to re-evaluate everything that he believes about himself. I know. I've been there. I wanted to give up. And now I want to inflict that on someone else. However prettily I wrap it up and however much I know and accept that it is for the best and will help him, I just don't know if I have the guts to hold his hand on the first few steps of that journey.

Will seeking out his demons to slay them awaken my own?

***

To: Mr X (X_Towers@hotmail.com)
From: Elise Waterford
(elise.waterford@monochrome.co.uk)

X,
I don't really know why I'm writing this email but you seem like a kind and good person and I don't really know who else to speak to about it. My boyfriend just agrees with everything I say, my boss will support whatever will help me get through the feature and I don't even know if my friends back home are reading my blog. Whoever you are, you seem genuine so I'm going to go out on a limb and trust you. I'm really struggling this week. I never thought it was going to be easy but I certainly never expected it to be so emotionally challenging and draining.

I didn't expect to see so many facets of myself in these men, especially Jim. He was so horrible, so abrasive. It scared me on a very deep level that I could so easily have turned out that way if I hadn't had help right when I needed it most. I've never talked about my experiences to anyone other than a counsellor and now, here I am, expecting him to confront his issues for the sake of some silly magazine feature. It seems so painfully hypocritical that I don't know if I can live with myself right now. I've spent the last hour crying over my stupid blog post. Are you there? Can we talk?
Elise

To: Elise Waterford
(elise.waterford@monochrome.co.uk)

From: Mr X (X_Towers@hotmail.com)

Elise,
Firstly, you can trust me absolutely. These
conversations are entirely confidential and will never be
seen by anyone other than me. Secondly, I have to be
honest and say my leaning is to push you to stick with it
because I enjoy reading your blog. It's funny and heart-
warming and you're really making a difference to these
guys. That said, if it's affecting you on this level then you
need to do what is best for you. If it's getting too much, and
this is not because you're tired or a long way from home,
then hand in your notice. I said I would be here for you to
talk to and I meant it. I'll try and give you an unbiased
opinion.

You've obviously been through some dark times in
your life and this project was bound to stir up some long
forgotten feelings. It's hard not to see yourself reflected in
the people around you. We're human. It's how we identify
ourselves...by looking for the familiarities in the people
around us. It makes us feel at home. Sometimes those
familiarities aren't positive. It's how you deal with the
situation that defines you, not the fact that you recognised
the darkness in you.
Ever yours,
X

To: Mr X (X_Towers@hotmail.com)
From: Elise Waterford
(elise.waterford@monochrome.co.uk)

X,
I don't believe in asking people to do things I wouldn't
do myself, so if how I deal with this situation is what defines
me then here is my confession.

I married young. I was 19 and we'd been together for 6 years, all through senior school and college. We did all those things that young couples do...started saving for a house, talked about starting a family. It was like some advert for marital bliss. Two years later Max was killed in a car crash. He'd been drink driving and none of it made any sense because he told me he'd been working late. I found out at the funeral that he'd been having an affair with not one, but two of my 'closest' friends. I stood there watching them put him in the ground and all I could think was that I wasn't just losing one person, I'd lost four. I'd lost my husband, my 'friends' and myself. They say that once something is seen it cannot be unseen. I lost my innocence that day. I couldn't believe I'd been so duped and so stupid. I wanted to crawl inside my own skin, driving myself crazy wondering how many of the people I had surrounded myself with knew about it, how many of them had been laughing at poor, stupid, loyal Elise behind my back.

At first I was angry and ashamed and then I ran the whole gamut of emotions from denial right through the grieving process. To accept it, I had to learn how I could have been so self-destructive that I ended up in that situation in the first place. It was a brutal process. I had to re-evaluate everything I thought I knew about myself and look at it deconstructed in the cold light of day. I nearly didn't make it through. Suicide crossed my mind more than once over those long and dark months but in the end I resisted the temptation and somehow came through to be the woman I am today.

I don't regret it. It's the only thing that's keeping me going this week. What I went through taught me the value of life and of love. I'm a stronger, better, more resilient person for having been through it and most days I'm glad I chose life.

*There. I've said it. I have trusted you in the same way
that Jim will have to trust me. I hope his journey is as
healing and strengthening as mine was and I hope I can do
him the justice that I had when I was going through it. I
don't know that confessing it helps, but I suppose I feel
closer to him now that we're in the same boat. Maybe that
will help me help him. Who knows?*
Elise

**To: Elise Waterford
(elise.waterford@monochrome.co.uk)
From: Mr X (X_Towers@hotmail.com)**

*Elise,
I don't know what to say that won't sound like a
cliché. Thank you for your honesty, for trusting me with your
secret. Suddenly your empathy and insight make more
sense.*

*All I will say is this – you have to understand and
experience the darkness to truly understand the light. I
won't pretend I know what it's like to walk through the
shadows that you have, but I can tell you that to stand
beside you is to bask in the radiance of your goodness. You
overflow with light. Whatever you feel, and however much
you regret or reflect that dark time in those around you,
that's not who you are any more. You have more joy in your
heart than almost anyone I've ever met in my life and in a
strange, twisted way that's something to be thankful for.*

*You should go call someone you love, someone in
your family. Eat some cake or, if you haven't got cake, eat
chocolate. Get warm and feel loved. You need some
downtime. I'll be up all night and I'll leave my computer on
if you want to talk again.*

Ever yours, in darkness and in light,
X

When Nathan stopped by that night he found Elise crying in the bath. There were empty chocolate wrappers all over the bathroom floor and a cold cup of tea on the side.

"Oh my God!" Shocked he grabbed a towel from the radiator and pulled her up into his arms. The water was freezing. She must have been sat there for a couple of hours at least. "Elise, what's wrong?" He lifted her bodily out of the bath and hustled her into the bedroom where he briskly towelled her down and pulled a dressing gown around her. "Speak to me sweetie, what's wrong?"

"I don't think I can do it." She sobbed. "It's so cruel."

"Do what?" Bewildered he helped her through to the kitchen and sat her at the table while he put the kettle on.

She explained through her tears that she had decided to organise an intervention for Jim. She had contacted all the women who had spoken to him online and asked them for a brief video account of why they had no interest in speaking to him again. Before she could help him she needed him to understand what the problem was, that his manner was too awful for anyone to want to love him. Only by accepting that he needed to change would he accept the help she had put into place for him and the manner of his accepting had to be so deep and profound that there was no way to do it gently. She had spoken to his parents and discovered that he had changed after a particularly messy break-up at the age of eighteen and that they thought a broken heart was the cause of his current attitude problem.

The only way she could fix him was to play him the videos of these women telling her exactly why they didn't like him and then put him through counselling to challenge the basis of his being, to try and change his way of behaving. But the videos were harrowing...the women were both blunt and honest and Elise knew that she wouldn't have the strength of character to sit and listen to anyone saying those things about her. And then the counselling...it would take him right back to the darkest days of his life and force him to examine them in detail.

"I can't do it to him. I can't." She wept over and over again. "Those videos are so hurtful. I can't do it. Not for some stupid magazine article."

"Listen to me." He gathered her into a hug. "You're not doing it for the article. You're doing it for him. If he hadn't been so lonely in his life he wouldn't have been internet dating in the first place. He's looking for a companion and you are trying to help him get one. No-one said that was going to be an easy or pleasant process and you know yourself that the last two weeks have been massively emotional for all concerned. The way I see it he has three choices. He either accepts the help you're offering him and goes through this process now, he continues the way he's living and faces it ten years down the line when it's so much more ingrained and inclined to be a lot worse, or he spends the rest of his life alone. Of the three of those I think your way is the least cruel."

"But I have to break him." She sobbed. "He has to be a broken man before I can put him back together and it will take weeks of counselling. I can't just do it over two days and then leave him to fend for himself."

"Can he afford the counselling?" Nathan asked and Elise shook her head.

"The magazine is paying for it. I've set it up through the expenses for the feature."

"Then you're not leaving him to fend for himself." It seemed simple to him. "You're still talking to Mark and Dave aren't you?"

"Yes." She snuffled but her tears seemed to be slowing down.

"So why should this be any different?" He reasoned. "He's going to continue getting the help he needs and you guys will still be speaking a week or a month or even a year from now. This is the opportunity of a lifetime for him."

"What if he hates me?" She snuffled, the sobs almost completely stopped by now.

"He might resent you at first." He wasn't going to lie to her. "But eventually he'll come to realise that you did the best you could for him and when he meets a woman he'll realise he has you to thank for it. You just need to make him understand before he starts that it's not going to be an easy process."

"That's a difficult conversation to have." She said quietly. "I don't know that anything I can say will prepare him for it."

"As long as you try." He rocked her gently, kissing the top of her head. "You're a good person Elise. He's in good hands." She took a long, deep and shuddering breath and then some of the tension flowed out of her. "Why don't you go and get into bed?" He suggested. "I'll bring you a cup of tea through. Do you want me to stay over?"

"Yes please." She still sounded miserable but she wasn't crying anymore and she obediently went through to the bedroom. A few moments later he heard the hair dryer start up.

He was just fishing the tea bag out of the mug when her mobile rang. It was charging on the kitchen worktop and she clearly couldn't hear it so he picked it up.

"Hello?"

"Nathan, it's Taylor. Is Elise there?" Nathan squashed down his jealousy.

"She's just drying her hair. I'll ask her to call you back."

"No it's okay. I just wanted to check she was okay. Her blog post wasn't her usual cheerful self."

"She's not." Nathan gritted his teeth. "I came in to find her crying in the bath surrounded by empty chocolate wrappers. This feature is really taking it out of her."

He could hear Taylor blowing out a long breath. "I had no idea."

"She'll be fine. I'll stay with her tonight." Nathan flexed his neck. "She's almost halfway through. This week has just been a tough one."

"Okay. Take my number from her phone. If it looks like it's getting too much then call me and we'll work something out."

"I will do." He had no intention of doing anything of the sort but he wasn't going to say that out loud. Taylor hung up without saying anything else and Nathan sighed, setting the phone back on the work top. He didn't want to wish the time they had together away but he would be glad when this first six weeks were over.

He carried Elise's cup of tea through to where she was just getting tucked under the covers. "Taylor called to check you were okay." He told her, handing it over.

"Did he want me to call him back?" She asked wearily and he shook his head.

"No. I told him you'd be fine."

"Okay." She snuggled in with her hot cup. "I'm sure he'll have sent me an email...I'll reply to it tomorrow."

"Will you be okay here for a while? I haven't eaten yet."

"I'll be fine. There's sandwich stuff in the fridge."

By the time he returned she was fast asleep, empty mug clasped loosely in her hand. Smiling, he rescued it from its precarious position and set it on the bedside table, stripping his clothes off and sliding in beside her. She stirred and he hushed her as she moved into his arms, after which he lay in the darkness listening to her sleep.

The following morning he hugged her at the door.

"Call me." He made her promise. "I'll keep my phone on. If it's too much then call me and I'll come find you."

"I will." She kissed him one last time and he headed out the door. He'd be back after work for them to go to dance class so she wouldn't be on her own for long. Taking a deep breath she grabbed her laptop and keys and headed out the door. It was time to face the music.

Chapter 9

Elise was deliberately not meeting Jim at his home. She didn't want him to associate any of the sadness or confusion of today with his own personal space so she had arranged for them to have a private office at the magazine headquarters. She asked at reception and was directed to an empty office where she set up her laptop ready to go and then waited for the phone call to say he was in the building.

When the phone finally did ring her heart skipped several beats and for a moment she was frozen, unwilling to answer it and set the ball rolling. Eventually she forced herself to pick it up and asked them to send him on up to the third floor where she was waiting.

Jim arrived looking a little grungy in a pair of skinny jeans and an indie T-shirt with leather wristbands on. It was a look that suited him. She greeted him and sat him down in front of the laptop, leaning against the table next to it as she wondered how to start. There wasn't really any way except honesty so she took a deep breath.

"Jim, I've asked you here today because I think I've figured out what the problem is but I think you're going to struggle with it and probably be a little hurt by it."

"Okay." He looked confused.

"The problem here is clearly with you, so I've organised an intervention. I have some videos I need you to watch and I have to be honest with you...they're brutal. You're not going to like what you hear, but I need you to hear it so that afterwards you're ready to start from scratch. This is a difficult journey I'm going to take you on and I need to know that you trust me before we start."

He looked uneasy. "Well, you got those other guys dates didn't you?"

"Yes, but their situations were different. I just need you to trust that I will help you through this and that I have everything in place to pick up the pieces."

"You're scaring me now." He tried to make light of it but Elise could feel her eyes prickling.

"Good. Because neither of us should undertake this lightly." She handed him a packet of tissues. "I'm going to be right outside in the hallway okay? I've seen them so I don't need to sit through them again. If it gets too much we can stop at any time."

Bewildered, he accepted the tissues and waited for her to start the program.

"I'll be right outside," she repeated as the first video started scrolling and walked for the door. As she left she heard the woman on the screen say 'Why wouldn't I contact Jim again? Because he's the most arrogant individual I've ever had the misfortune to speak to...' The door closing cut her off and Elise leaned against the wall heaving for breath and hoping that she'd done the right thing.

"Are you okay?" A young woman heading past stopped, her face full of concern, and Elise nodded.

"I'll be fine. Really."

"Okay." She didn't look convinced. "But you sure look like you could use a cup of coffee. Canteen is that way." She pointed somewhere away down the corridor and tottered off in her skyscraper heels.

"Thanks." Elise called to her retreating back and the woman waved a hand in acknowledgement. She wasn't to know that Elise couldn't go anywhere. There was almost half an hour's worth of videos and she didn't know if Jim could bear to watch them all. Her phone rang and she fished it out of her pocket, seeing with relief that it was Nathan's face on the display.

"How's it going?" He asked quietly.

"I don't know." She closed her eyes and leaned her head back against the wall. "I just started him on the videos. I was just trying to decide if he's going to watch them all."

"I suspect he will." His voice was so kind it made her throat ache with unshed tears. "Do you have someone to be with you?"

"I promised him I'd be right outside the door in case it's too much." She told him. "I can't just go wandering off."

"Fair point." He sighed. "For what it's worth, I think you're doing the right thing."

"I hope so." She checked her watch. "The counsellor is due in a little under an hour so he won't have long to wait when the videos finish. Help will be right here."

"Good." He sighed. "I have to get back to work. I just wanted to check you were okay."

"I'm fine." She smiled despite the ache in her throat. "I love you."

"Not as much as I love you my beautiful senorita." His voice was full of warmth and her smile widened. Their dance class on Tuesday had been just as much fun as the first one had been.

"I'm looking forward to dance class tonight." She murmured and she could hear him chuckling.

"Me too. I'll have to go home after work to get my kit so I'll meet you at the studio. When are you going to be photographed? I thought that was this week sometime."

"Damn it!" Elise had totally forgotten. "It's tomorrow afternoon. I'm so glad you reminded me. I'll have to go after I've been to the office to get the outfit."

"Well that's okay. You'll have plenty of time. Why don't you come and stay over with me tonight after dance class. We'll get a takeaway and relax some."

"Sounds perfect." She smiled. "See you later."

They hung up and she slipped the phone back into her pocket, checking the time again. He'd only been in there five minutes. It was going to be a really long half hour.

Ten minutes later she was pacing up and down the hallway when Taylor appeared from the direction of the lifts carrying a couple of take-out cups of coffee.

"Ella said I might find you here." He greeted, kissing her cheek. "I didn't believe her but then here you are. What are you doing?"

"Carrying out an intervention." She responded drily. "Behind that door is a man listening to some extremely unpleasant things about himself. I was too chicken to watch. Who's Ella?"

"One of my secretaries. She said she saw you down here a few minutes ago."

"Ah." Elise nodded. "Young woman, tall shoes?"

He laughed. "Sounds about right. She said you looked in need of coffee." He offered her one of the cardboard cups and Elise accepted it gratefully, savouring the rich dark aroma that took her away from her worries for a few short moments.

"Thanks. Thank Ella for me too."

"I will." He leaned against the wall opposite her. "So how brutal is this intervention exactly? Do I need to worry about a lawsuit?"

"Depends." Elise rubbed the back of her neck. "How would you take to being told by several women over the course of half an hour that you were arrogant, judgemental, unpleasant to be around and generally unlikeable?"

"Wow...that is harsh." He looked a little worried. "Is he really that bad?"

Elise nodded. "After an hour with him I wanted to slap him."

"That's totally not like you." He seemed surprised. "He must be bad."

Elise shrugged. "I don't know. I think it's a defence mechanism. There's a good guy somewhere underneath all the arrogance and vanity, I just know it. But until he can accept he has a problem he can't fix it."

"Hence the intervention...?"

"Yeah." She started pacing again. "But I've got a counsellor coming straight afterwards to help him work through his feelings on it."

"That's good." He watched her pace in silence for a while. "Can you come up to the office when you're done here?" He asked suddenly. "It'd be nice to sit down and have a proper chat with you."

"Sure." It seemed he was going to be friendly again today and Elise risked a cautious smile. "I'll come up while he's in with the counsellor. It'll be an hour long session and it's private so I can't sit in on it unless he specifically asks me to."

"Okay." He flashed her one of his dazzling smiles. "I'll get back to work, but I'll see you in a little while. Just take the lift to the twelfth floor and you can't miss my office. It's got my name on the door."

"Will do." She held up her cup. "Thanks for the coffee."

"You're welcome." She watched him stride away down the hallway admiring the cut of his suit. It really was beautiful and probably cost more than she earned in a year. The thought was entirely depressing.

When the half hour was up and she'd given him a good ten minutes to compose himself, Elise went back into the office. Jim was sat staring at the empty screen, his face pale and his eyes red.

"Are you okay?" She asked softly and he turned to her slowly as though rousing from sleep.

"I had no idea." His voice was gravelly and he cleared his throat as he really looked at her. "I thought I was being clever. And manly." Suddenly he looked lost and his face seemed to crumple in on itself. "Am I really that bad?"

She didn't want to hurt him but lying would have made it even worse. "I wouldn't have come for a second date." She tried to be diplomatic about it. "It's a little hard to find someone attractive when they keep putting you down all the time."

"I had no idea." He repeated as his eyes wandered back to the screen. "I really didn't know." And then he started crying. Elise rushed to him and hugged him as he let it all out. When the phone rang it startled both of them and he plucked a tissue to dry his eyes as Elise answered it.

The counsellor had arrived slightly early and Elise asked them to send him straight on up. "I booked a counsellor for you." She told Jim gently. "I figured that after the videos you'd need someone to talk it through with. He'll be here for an hour today, but I've booked you in for ten sessions so, before he goes, you can organise times with him. It's all paid for by the magazine."

He was too emotional to answer so Elise just squeezed his shoulder and waited with him for the counsellor to arrive. When the guy got there, he set himself up with a notepad and pen and introduced himself to Elise and Jim and then Elise left them to it, noting the time on her watch so she knew when to come back down.

Following Taylor's instructions, she took the lift to the twelfth floor and looked around. To the left was a small ante room with two desks in it, one of which Ella was sat behind, clacking away at her keyboard, and beyond it was an oak door with Taylor's name on it.

Catching her eye, Ella stopped typing. "Go right on through." She said with a smile. "He's expecting you."

"Thanks." Smiling awkwardly at her and feeling a bit rumpled in her jeans and blouse, Elise knocked on Taylor's door and pushed through when he answered.

"Hey." His smile really was dazzling, all perfectly even teeth and brilliance. "Take a seat. You want another coffee?"

"Yes please." She did as she was told and took a seat in one of the plush chairs across from his desk, taking a moment to admire the palatial office. "Guess being an editor entitles you to an office the size of a football field huh?" She joked and he grinned.

"You should see it the night before we go to press. It's packed in here with everyone shouting. That's why I need a big office."

"Fair enough." She accepted the coffee he made her, in a proper mug this time, and relaxed into the seat.

"So how did the intervention go?" He asked and she slumped.

"About as expected." She tried to pull herself together. "He was pretty devastated, kept telling me he had no idea. He cried. A lot."

"But he's with the counsellor now?" He prompted and she nodded.

"Yeah. Fingers crossed this will be a breakthrough for him."

"I'm sure it will." He smiled encouragingly and for a few moments they sat in silence, sipping their coffee and waiting for the other to speak. He spoke first, setting his mug on his desk. "Elise, I have to know before we go to the ball tomorrow night...why didn't you reply to any of my emails?"

"Which emails?" Elise stared at him. "I've replied to every email you sent me."

"No, the ones I sent after we met in Aviemore." He frowned. "I must have sent you at least ten and you never replied to any of them."

Elise was floored. "I didn't get any emails from you after Aviemore. I thought you were ignoring me and then I came here and you gave me the cold shoulder."

"That doesn't make any sense." He stared at her. "You have the same email address. I'm sure I've used your personal address at least once since you started working here. I know I typed it in right. I was cold towards you because I thought you'd ignored me but then you were so friendly when you started submitting the blogs and I got confused... But even if you didn't get my emails, why didn't you return any of my calls?"

Her jaw dropped. "You never called me Taylor. I swear on my life I never had a single call or missed call from you."

"But I..." His gaze suddenly went blank as whatever he was about to say caught up with him. "Oh my God." Blinking, he turned to his computer for several minutes and then his face turned thunderous. "They were all recalled." Icy didn't even begin to describe his voice. He pressed the intercom. "Ella, get in here now."

"Right away Mr Stone."

Elise heard her footsteps and then the door opened. Ella looked nervous and Elise could totally understand why. Taylor looked fit to be tied.

"On whose orders did you cut off contact between me and Elise?" He demanded.

She flushed beet red. "It wasn't-"

"I know you all had to be in on it. These emails were sent at all times of the day, so all four of you must have been checking and recalling them. And I know you've all been on duty when I asked you to get Elise on the phone and every one of you has lied and told me she wasn't answering her phone when in actual fact you weren't calling her at all."

It all suddenly made a horrible kind of sense, why she'd had no emails or missed calls, and Elise felt sick as she watched Ella start to cry. "It was your brother." Ella confessed shakily. "He told us if we didn't, he'd make sure we got sacked."

"Anton did this?" Taylor seemed shocked but Ella nodded meekly.

"I'm so sorry, Mr Stone. I didn't want to. She seemed so nice." The tears were flowing freely now. "I didn't know what to do, but he was adamant and then I saw her in the corridor today and I thought maybe if I told you she was there you could meet up and Anton couldn't say it was my fault and everything would work out okay."

She paused to snatch a breath and for the first time Taylor's features softened slightly. "It's okay. He should never have threatened you. But you are my secretary and I wouldn't have let him sack you," he told her sternly. "I'll forgive you for the service you did Elise this morning, but don't ever lie to me again."

"No sir, I won't. I swear. I'm so sorry. You're the best boss I've ever had." She fled the office weeping and Taylor got up to pace around like a caged lion.

"I don't get it." He muttered to himself. "I just don't get it." Finally he stopped and picked up the phone, stabbing a number in with angry hands. He didn't even give the person at the other end a chance to say hello. "Get Anton down here now," he demanded. "He's got some explaining to do." He slammed the phone back in its cradle and it almost slid off the edge of the desk.

"Your brother works here as well?" Elise asked, more to try and break up the tension before a fight broke out than anything else, and Taylor nodded as he continued to pace.

"Our father owns the company that owns the magazine. We've both worked in the journalism industry since we were teenagers."

"I didn't know."

"Most people don't." A flash of bitter amusement twitched across his lips. "We both got to where we are today through hard graft and harder work. But when daddy owns the company there are plenty who assume it's nepotism at its worst."

"You're great at your job." Elise pointed out. "Surely no-one can doubt that?"

A genuine smile this time. "Bless you...your heart is so innocent."

She was about to respond when his office door opened again, this time without a knock, and a man stepped through who was clearly his brother. The family resemblance was striking. "Taylor what's this ab-..." He caught sight of Elise. "Oh."

"Well you might say 'oh'." In an instant all of Taylor's rage had come flooding to the fore again. "What on earth were you thinking?"

Anton sighed. "Taylor, you came back from your skiing trip and you wouldn't shut up about this damn woman. It was 'Elise this' and 'Elise that' constantly. I'm your brother. I know you better than anyone else and I knew that if I didn't step in and divert this disaster, there was a very real chance you'd fall for this woman."

Taylor's jaw dropped. "What?" Elise was just as stunned.

Anton kicked the door closed. "Taylor, you sounded infatuated, like a teenager with a crush. But she's not of our world. Look at her." He waved a dismissive hand in her general direction and she shrank inwards with shame. "You need to be courting someone from your own class who would fit in with the social circles we move in. You can't go dating some nobody from the sticks. And God forbid you ever married her." He said it with such disgust that Elise felt nauseous.

"Some nobody from the sticks?" The words had hit Taylor hard. "How dare you? Have you even looked at the figures for the last fortnight? Hits on the site have increased by more than tenfold."

"It's not about figures!" Anton threw his hands up. "You cannot date this woman. Look at her. Look at her!" His lip curled in a sneer. "She probably buys her clothes at the supermarket and this is who you want to be seen with in the society pages?"

None of them knew who was surprised more when Taylor landed a punch that sent Anton sprawling across the floor.

"Fuck!" Anton touched a trembling hand to his face and gaped at the blood on his fingers. "You broke my nose."

"This woman is worth more than ten of you." Taylor was so angry he was actually shaking with fury. "Get out of my office. Get out!"

"You wait until I tell father about this!" Anton staggered to his feet and left the office, stumbling slightly as he reeled from the hit.

"Are you okay?" Elise ventured cautiously as Taylor stared at the door with mixed emotions visibly warring on his face.

"No. I'm not." The fight seemed to go out of him and he slumped in his chair. "I'm sorry, Elise, but could you give me some time alone?"

"Of course." She instantly got up and set her coffee mug by the machine. "Um...I'm sorry." She walked behind the desk and hugged him briefly.

"Don't be. It's not your fault." He squeezed her quickly before letting her go. "And don't pay any attention to those awful things he said. It's not about what's on the outside, it's about what's on the inside. You're one of the most amazing people I know."

"Thanks." Embarrassed now, she left the office quickly. Ella was staring wide-eyed down the hall after Anton, but she looked contrite when Elise emerged.

"I really am sorry," she apologised. "I didn't realise you guys liked each other and I was so worried."

"It's okay." Elise paused by her desk. "It's not like that – we're just friends, but we'll work it out. There's no harm done."

"Good." The secretary smiled shyly. "I read your blog. It's funny."

"Thanks." Elise managed to smile. "You're the first person apart from my boyfriend I know that actually reads it."

"We all do." Feeling more comfortable now Ella leaned back from her desk. "Those poor guys...they're so clueless. We love the feature." Suddenly she gasped. "Do you know who Mr X is? It's sooooo romantic!"

"I haven't got a clue." Elise smiled uncomfortably. "He could be anyone but he can leave me all the love letters he wants. I'm already involved with someone."

"That's a shame." She looked really disappointed. "It would have made a great love story – you helping all these guys to find love and then you find love through the same feature."

"That's true." She had to admit it would have had a certain poetic justice. "But never mind. I'm sure Mr X will get over it and find someone else to love."

"I hope so."

Elise checked her watch again. "I have to go – project 3 is almost ready for me."

"Ooh, good luck!" Ella smiled at her and Elise felt herself warming towards her.

"Thanks. I'm sure I'll see you around."

"I hope so!" Ella waved as she headed out the door and Elise stepped into the lift feeling like she was leaving the Twilight Zone. She hoped she never went through anything as awkward as the confrontation she had just witnessed but she had the horrible feeling that it was all just the beginning.

Jim left the magazine offices a changed man. They went for a quiet lunch together while he struggled to make sense of some of the emotions storming through him. The counselling had helped, but it would be a long and difficult journey and Elise's heart ached for him.

"She broke my heart," he confessed suddenly as their salads arrived. "I never told anyone."

"A girl you were dating?" Elise didn't want to let on how much his mother had known or guessed.

"We met when we were fifteen and dated for three years." He looked dazed as he relayed this. "I thought we were going to go to university together and then get married. It was all planned." He studied his plate like it had landed from another planet. "It was all *planned*." He whispered again.

"Life doesn't always follow the path we think it will." Elise winced inwardly, realising she sounded like some tuppence guru, but he didn't seem to notice.

"When we were eighteen, she told me she was pregnant. I was so happy I thought I'd burst."

Wow...now that was something his mother hadn't known and Elise was shocked. "What happened?" She questioned gently and his face crumpled again.

"She got rid of it. Just like that. I begged her not to, but she told me she was too young, she had too many plans."

"Oh Jim." She didn't know what to say. "I'm so sorry." She reached across and took his hand as tears spilled onto them.

"All I ever wanted was to teach kids music but now when I look at them I can't help wondering what my little boy or girl would have been like if they'd lived."

She couldn't even begin to imagine how painful it must be for him. This unnamed girl hadn't just taken away his child and broken his heart, she'd taken away his dreams and his future, condemned him to being tortured by the one thing he had always wanted. No wonder he had become a cold shell around the ruins of his heart. It was incredible he'd stayed on track at the school.

"I'm sure your child would have been beautiful." She squeezed his hand. As if realising she was there for the first time he straightened up and scrubbed the tears from his face.

"I'm sorry." He looked embarrassed. "I never told anyone that before. I don't know why it suddenly came out."

"Sometimes it's just the right time to let it out." Elise smiled encouragingly at him. "Once the first telling is past it becomes a lot easier to say it again."

"The counselling will help." He picked up his fork and pushed his food around his plate for a little while, clearly without much appetite. "I need to let her go, don't I?" He asked suddenly and Elise nodded.

"Yes, Jim. You do. Once you stop wrapping yourself around with your rage and sorrow you'll find new dreams and new children to mend your heart."

"You think?" His smile was bright under his red-rimmed eyes and Elise nodded seriously.

"Yes I do. With all my being."

They spent the afternoon at his flat ritually burning everything of his ex-girlfriend's that he had retained for the last five years. It was something better suited to teenage girls, but Jim seemed to find the process immensely cathartic and Elise wasn't going to argue with him. They lit a fire in a bucket in the back yard of his tiny tenement building and burned photographs by the hundred, a couple of items of clothing, small gifts she had given him in their time together such as books and CDs. It took them almost two hours.

"I feel better now." Jim raised his arms to the sky and stretched and Elise couldn't help but wonder. He might be streaked with soot and dust, but he looked a lighter man than he had when he had walked into the office that morning. "Definitely better." He grinned at her. "I feel free."

By the time she had made sure he was happy to be on his own and rushed home to shower and change and get rid of the smell of smoke, Elise was almost late to dance class. She rushed in to the dance school, skidding round the corner with her overnight bag flapping, and Nathan's face lit up as he laughed.

"I thought you weren't coming." He chided and she heaved for breath.

"Wouldn't miss it for the world. Had a crazy day." She managed between gasps. "Am I late?"

He checked his watch. "No, you got here with a couple of minutes to spare. Why don't you go grab a cup of water?" She did as he suggested and they went through to the studio. It was full of people all milling around and they took their place in a small clear area for the warm up stretches. They were clearly the newest students and felt a bit awkward as they circled the room along with everyone else. They were encouraged by everyone though and the tutors followed them closely, instructing and correcting, so they didn't have too many mishaps.

Afterwards as they walked towards the tube station Nathan put an arm around her. "You seem preoccupied." He told her. "You want to talk about it?"

"Not now. I want to eat some grossly unhealthy food and spend some time cuddling on your couch before I even start telling you about my day."

He grinned. "I'm pretty sure I could help you with that."

Later when they were snuggling up together surrounded by Chinese takeout carton carnage Elise told him about her day, starting with Jim.

"That's awful!" He gasped when she told him the cause of Jim's heartache. "I can't believe she'd just get rid of it like that!"

"Me either." Elise shuddered. "I can understand her not wanting to keep it if the time wasn't right for her but if he wanted it...what a mess."

"Poor guy."

"And for him not to tell anyone what he was going through." The thought of keeping all that inside made her chest ache. "His mother had no idea. None of them did. They thought he was just cut up about the break up."

"Not surprising he turned out so abrasive." Nathan commented. "But at least he's getting help now. This feature might just be the best thing that ever happened to him."

"I wanted to tell him that today was the first day of the rest of his life but then I remembered saying that same thing to Mark." Elise sighed.

"It would still have been right. In both their cases." Nathan kissed the top of her head. "It is the first day of the rest of his life."

"How did I end up here?" She asked miserably. "I don't have any training or background in this and somehow I've ended up playing God in these men's lives."

"You don't need training to be a good person." He shrugged. "You're over thinking this. All you can do is your best." He squeezed her reassuringly. "So what else happened today?"

"I found out why Taylor was so rude to me when I came down and he broke his brother's nose because of it."

"What?" Nathan was astonished. "Taylor broke his brother's nose?"

"Yup." Elise was still a bit bemused by it all. "Laid him out flat right there on the office floor."

"You're going to have to start at the beginning with this story." Nathan was incredulous. "This I have to hear."

"Apparently when Taylor came back from Aviemore he told his brother about me and Anton got the wrong end of the stick. He thought we were more than just friends and figured it would be damaging to Taylor's reputation to be dating some penniless nobody with a terrible fashion sense. So he threatened Taylor's secretaries into sabotaging our friendship by recalling his emails and faking phone calls. Taylor thought I'd been ignoring him which is why he was so rude to me when I arrived."

Nathan's jaw had dropped. "Two things...one, you are not a penniless nobody and there's nothing at all wrong with your fashion sense. You always look beautiful. Two, how did this end up in a broken nose?"

"Taylor figured it out and got his secretary to confess so he called Anton down to the office." She shifted uncomfortably. "Anton said some less than gentlemanly things about me and Taylor was defending my honour."

"How very gentlemanly." To her surprise Nathan didn't sound at all irritated, just amused. "Did he really break his nose?"

"It certainly looked broken. There was blood all down his shirt." Elise had to smile at the memory of Anton's face as he lay on the floor.

"Excellent." He sounded satisfied. "Remind me to shake his hand next time we meet. I don't appreciate anyone that puts you down."

"Is this a man thing?" Elise asked amused and Nathan grinned.

"Something like that. I'd have knocked his lights out if I'd been there, saved Taylor the trouble." He said easily and Elise burst out laughing.

"Definitely a man thing." She shook her head.

"Do I want to know what he said about you?" Nathan asked a few moments later and Elise shifted again as another small pang of hurt shot through her.

"No." She said after a moment's hesitation. "It doesn't matter anyway. He won't say it in front of either of us again. Anyway, I pity him. It's a sad world to live in when you feel you have to judge everyone by the clothes they wear and the size of their bank accounts rather than the person they actually are. I wonder if he has ever actually loved or been loved."

"Probably not." He blew out a breath. "You're right. That is a sad existence." He fluffed her hair. "How did you get to be so wise, huh?"

She burst out laughing. "It's the love of a good man, I'm sure."

They say that the evil men do lives after them but the good is oft interred with their bones. I wonder how many of us think about how our actions impact on the world around us...how a word or a deed can live for years in the lives of the people we come into contact with. I'm not talking about those silly little every day decisions like whether or not to wear that lime green spandex or which channel to watch. I'm not even talking about the few pounds you did or didn't give to charity when you had the opportunity. I'm talking about how many of us actually mean it when we say "I love you". How many of us choose our fear of ridicule or need to associate only with people from our social circle over our hearts when it comes to life decisions? How many of us are in a relationship where we make our own decisions without consulting our other halves?

How many of you have made a decision that has broken a heart...broken a person? And how many of you are brave or self-aware enough to realise it?

Jim is a broken man, broken by the selfishness of others. He's like an old sock that someone poked a massive hole in the heel of, and he patched it and darned it and got it twisted right up into being almost unwearable, when really it just needed unravelling and re-knitting. He didn't realise that the shell he had created to protect himself was working too well...it was pushing people away. It fell to me to take him apart so that he could be reconstructed.

I organised an intervention. It was one of the hardest things I've ever done. To be kind I had to be cruel, and it hurt. It really hurt. I had to sit him in a room to listen to the truth about his behaviour from women that had experienced it. Many of the women he had dated gave me videos of them explaining why they wouldn't contact him again. To fix him I had to break him. And boy did I break him. Bless his brave soul, he sat through it all and took every painful moment of it to heart. It was so brutal I had arranged counselling for him afterwards...a ten week course. I'm still not sure if that will be enough to help him work through his issues.

I thought he would hate me, but he didn't. After the intervention and first counselling session, we went for lunch together followed by an afternoon at his house. He was a totally different person. Gone were the arrogance and pretentiousness, leaving in their place a strangely humble man who was ready to start over. He had finally let go and underneath that glacial exterior was someone warm and most definitely human.

Only time will tell whether my intervention has helped on the dating front, but if the man I spent the afternoon with sticks around, I strongly suspect it won't be long before he finds love. There was a lot about him to like. I hope he will forgive me for what I have put him through in the weeks and months to come and I also hope he will invite me to a future wedding and, fingers crossed, many christenings!

If he was a cake, what would he be? Only one choice......a Baked Alaska.

When she opened up her inbox later that evening there was a one liner from Taylor in the internal mail system.

Dearest Elise, What on earth is a Baked Alaska??? Taylor xx

Grinning, she hit reply.

Taylor, It's a layer of sponge cake and a layer of ice cream surrounded by meringue. It gets baked in a really hot oven very quickly so the ice cream doesn't melt. Very difficult to make but one of my favourite desserts. If you've ever had it at one of your posh restaurants it would be known as a glace au four. Elise xx

Dearest Elise, I have never had such a thing. I will most certainly be on the look-out for it though. Sounds delicious. Have fun at the office today. I'll be away at meetings this afternoon but they're expecting you for your dress and I've also got a team from the makeover department ready to do your hair and make-up. I know you have an appointment with Mark at the studio so they'll leave you plenty of time. See you later xx

Elise stared at Taylor's last email wondering how on earth he had known she had an appointment to be photographed that afternoon. She certainly hadn't told him and suspected somebody at the studio must have said something. That was weird.

Shaking it off she checked the time and realised she was going to have to get going. If she was expected to have her hair and face done before her photo shoot then that only gave her a couple of hours and she had no idea what to expect on the outfit front. If she had to come home to collect shoes and a coat then she would be running late to catch Taylor back at the offices.

She arrived at the offices on time for her hair and make-up appointments ahead of the ball and reception were expecting her. They sent her straight to the fourth floor where the most flamboyantly camp man she had ever met gathered her up in a flurry of air kisses and polka dots and swept her into his domain.

"What a gorgeous figure you have!" He trilled happily as he flicked through rails of gowns. His name was Dominic and Elise couldn't help but smile as she followed him through the clothes. It was like stepping into Narnia. He heaped gown after gown into her arms, in a flurry of bright colours and expensive fabrics. When she didn't think she could carry any more he escorted her into a screened off area and helped her into dress after dress. He had barely done most of them up before dismissing them and moving onto the next one.

Finally he sucked in a breath and stepped back to take in the full effect. Elise was so exhausted and hot from getting dressed and undressed so many times, she almost didn't notice the look on his face.

"This one." He said reverently. "Roberto Cavalli. The genius. Flatterer of women everywhere."

"This one?" Elise looked down at the dress. It was a one shoulder asymmetric affair in sapphire blue velvet and satin. She had to admit it was gorgeous and her mind shied away from even daring to consider how much it cost.

"Yes. This one. Now..." he pursed his lips. "...shoes." He drew the word out as he grasped her hand and dragged her, dress and all, into a separate aisle. "What size are you?"

"Six."

"Excellent." He perused a rack of shoes in various colours, checking sizes and holding some pairs up against the dress before dismissing them. Finally he settled on a gorgeous pair of sparkling silver strapped heels. Elise had to hold the dress up while he laced them up for her. "Perfect." He grinned broadly, took her hand and dragged her off into another aisle to study accessories.

Half an hour later with a cluster of charm bangles, a deconstructed pearl necklace, a mother of pearl clutch, a new pair of almost invisible briefs and a jewelled hair comb, Elise was off to the sixth floor to the make-up department where they got people ready for photo shoots in the magazine. Dominic had allowed her to change back into her own clothes and the dress was busy being pressed and steamed for her return after she'd been to the studio.

They made her shower with expensive products and then she sat in a bathrobe in front of a giant mirror as they primped her hair and painted her face. By the time she was done she felt and looked a million dollars. Her skin had an alabaster perfection she'd never noticed and her hair was pinned up in loose curls, accented by the jewelled comb.

"You have two hours." The make-up artist warned her sternly. "Then you must be back here, in your dress, ready for a touch up before Mr Stone takes you to the ball."

"I feel like Cinderella." She muttered as she accepted the warning and headed downstairs back out into the street. It was a warm day in the city so she took her time heading over to the studio, not wanting to get hot and sweaty or melt her make-up.

When she arrived, Mark kissed her on both cheeks. "You look amazing!" He congratulated her. "Is this for the ball tonight?"

"Yeah." She blushed and was grateful for the air conditioning in the studio. "How are you doing?"

"Excellent thanks." He grinned, ushering her into a large white expanse. "I've got another date this weekend and I'm pretty hopeful about this one."

"That's awesome news!" Elise was delighted for him. "Well, you have my number so you'd better call or text and let me know how it went."

"I will." He chuckled. "You're like the fairy godmother of internet dating."

Elise burst out laughing. "I don't have a wand." She protested jokingly and he shrugged.

"I'll get you one." He sat her on a stool and stepped behind his camera, focusing on her face. "I saw on your blog that you're having a tough week this week."

"Yeah." She agreed quietly, all humour forgotten. "It was pretty brutal."

"Brutal but necessary." He reassured her. "I haven't seen today's post yet. How did it go?"

"About as well as could be expected." She sighed. "I have to give him credit – he took it a lot better than I would have. He accepted it too. He could have brushed it off but he didn't...he took it to heart and went into the counselling with an open mind."

"That's good." He adjusted a light. "So you're hopeful for him?"

"Yeah I am." She smiled a little sadly. "I think it'll be a few weeks before he's really ready to let go and date again properly but I'm sure he'll get there."

"That's good." He smiled at her. "So...any idea who this Mr X is yet?"

Elise frowned slightly. "Not a clue." She tucked her hair behind her ear. "It could be anyone."

"Is there anyone you are hoping it might be?" He asked with a cheeky twinkle and Elise chuckled.

"No."

He stopped what he was doing and stared at her. "Why, you're blushing!! Spill the beans!"

She giggled and shrugged. "I met someone. What can I say?"

"What's his name? Where does he work? Come on, I want details!" He stepped behind the camera again as Elise laughed.

"His name is Nathan and he works at my local library here. I met him my first day in the city. He's taking me to dance classes."

"Really?" He seemed surprised by that. "What kind of dance classes?"

"Argentine tango first but maybe other kinds afterwards." Some of the joy went out of her. "It depends what happens when I go back home. I only have another seven weeks here."

"Well how serious is it?" He asked. "You must have some idea by now."

"It's serious." A smile tugged at her mouth. "I love him to bits. Feels like we've known each other forever but three weeks isn't long enough to know all there is to know about a person."

"It's long enough to know your heart." He grinned at her. "It's kinda sweet that you came here to fix our love lives and ended up fixing yours too."

"I know." Amused she let him make fun of her for a little while.

Eventually he stepped out from behind the camera. "That's it." He told her and her jaw dropped.

"That's it? I didn't even know you were taking pictures!"

He burst out laughing. "It's a really quiet camera. The joys of digital."

"Oh. I see." She blinked, a little nonplussed. "When do I get to see the pictures?"

"Give me a couple of days at least." He helped her down off the stool. "I'll call you when they're ready."

"Awesome." She checked her watch. "I'd better run. The make-up artist is like a drill sergeant. If I'm not dressed, present and correct within the two hours she gave me I fear I'll be on the receiving end of a severe rollicking."

"On you go." He gestured her away. "I'll speak to you soon." She reached up to kiss his cheek and hurried out into the late afternoon.

She made it with a few minutes to spare and they brushed and polished her until she didn't even look like herself any more. When Taylor came down to collect her looking dashing in his tuxedo he whistled softly through his teeth and clapped his hands together admiringly.

"You look incredible." He complimented her.

"Looking rather fine yourself, boss." She winked at him and laughed as he kissed her hand. "Do I need a coat or something?" She asked when he was done doing his gentlemanly thing and he shook his head, tucking her arm through his as they walked down the hall.

"No. The car is right outside and it'll drop us off right at the door. A car will take you home later as well."

"Thanks." She allowed herself to be escorted into the back of a large luxury car and they pulled away from the kerb. "Where is this charity ball?" She asked as the city passed by and Taylor looked up from his phone.

"Wembley Arena."

"Oh my God!" She snapped her jaw shut as it dropped. "That place is huge! How big is this event?"

He grinned dazzlingly at her. "As big as it gets."

Elise's heart sank into her shoes when they arrived and she saw the bank of photographers and journalists arrayed by an expanse of red carpet that seemed a mile long.

"Don't worry, I'll be right here." Taylor told her warmly as he got out of his side of the car. Elise was going to open her own door but there was somebody there already and by the time she'd swung her feet over the sill of the door Taylor had arrived to take her hand and help her out. It felt like arriving on another planet. She was so blinded by the dazzle of camera flashes that she was grateful for the hand Taylor placed in the small of her back to guide her about. "Keep smiling." He whispered into her ear and she did as he suggested, pasting on a big smile as he shepherded her about, pausing here and there for photographers to catch posed photographs.

By the time they made it inside Elise's jaw was aching and she was so blinded she had to stop by the doors for a moment to allow her eyes to adjust.

"You did great." Taylor whispered to her. "Come on, we have to go and mingle." He escorted her around, introducing her to various people from the magazine but also to several celebrities. When they actually sat down at a table to eat she was so dazzled and star struck she could barely string three words together and sat silently as she ate, a little dazed by it all.

After the dinner there was an auction and a few speeches, after which a band struck up playing and Taylor got to his feet.

"May I have this dance?" He asked her charmingly and she blushed, unable to refuse.

"Of course." Taking the proffered hand she allowed herself to be led onto the dance floor and he took her in his arms.

"Do you know how to waltz?" He asked and she shook her head.

"I've seen it done but I've never tried it." She admitted. "I know the count though."

"You'll be fine. Just start stepping back on your right foot and follow my lead. Be pliant in my arms and I'll do the rest."

"Okay." A little dubiously she let him count her in and then allowed herself to be swept away into the throng of people.

At first it was awkward but after a few tunes she relaxed into his arms and they moved easily and gracefully around the floor. Taylor seemed to be nodding and smiling at everyone he recognised around them but Elise was too conscious of the hand pressed warmly in the expanse of bare skin below her shoulder blades. She'd never really understood before that the waltz was an intimate dance, a pressing together of two bodies moving in union. She was acutely aware of each bend and flex of his muscles as he moved her around and the scent of his cologne was heady in their tiny quiet space in amidst the crush of people. It was hard to resist the urge to lean her head against his chest and listen to his heartbeat.

"Are you okay?" He leaned down and murmured in her ear as they moved fluidly into their fifth dance. "I feel like I could keep going all night but if you're tired we can stop?"

"No I'm enjoying it." She turned to smile at him and her lips brushed his cheek by accident. She hadn't realised he was still so close. He stilled slightly as the air between them heated. Their mouths were so close together...a kiss was only a hairsbreadth away and the electric frisson built until it was an almost tangible presence.

"Elise." He breathed and it snapped her out of the spell.

"God, I'm sorry!" She flushed bright red and turned her face away. "I don't know what I was thinking...Nathan! Oh my god!"

"It's okay." He laughed easily. "I don't know what you were thinking but nothing actually happened. What Nathan doesn't know can't hurt him."

"I'm sorry, it must be the champagne." She continued, aware that he might feign amusement but he was breathing raggedly. What the hell had just happened? How did they go from being friends one moment to that almost raw hunger in the next? It made no sense. He was a great guy and maybe in another life, another world, they could be together, but she had made commitments in the here and now that she couldn't ignore. She felt swallowed with guilt for even wanting to feel his lips on hers, on her skin, on her neck...the thought made the blood rush to her cheeks anew and she fought to regain her composure.

"Are we going to talk about this?" He asked eventually when she had been quiet for a while and she shook her head resolutely.

"No. There's nothing to talk about."

"Come with me." He released her from hold and took her hand, leading her through the throngs of people swaying about on the dance floor. She thought about resisting but it might have looked a little odd so she allowed herself to be led to a small alcove behind some drapes.

"There's nothing to talk about." She repeated firmly before he could say a word. "I'd had too much champagne and I was carried away with the music."

"That's not true and you know it." He challenged. "You wanted to kiss me as much as I wanted to kiss you."

"It's not going to happen, Taylor." She wasn't going to lie and say she hadn't wanted him but it was too messy to contemplate. "I'm with Nathan. We're happy together. Whatever that was out there on the dance floor, it was a moment of craziness and it won't be repeated."

"I respect your views when it comes to Nathan, but don't discount me." He said seriously. "I've got a lot of making up to do after what Anton put us through."

"We've both got making up to do," she admitted wearily. "I should have known you wouldn't have just cut off all contact with me. I should have tried harder to call you. But all of that is as friends. As a professional, as a woman, as someone who can't deal with complicated right now, I just want to be your friend. No more, no less. Can you give me that?"

For a long moment he studied her and then he sighed. "For now. Whatever happens or doesn't happen, you'll always have my friendship." He raised her hand to his lips and laid a gentle kiss on the back of it. "Always."

Chapter 10

"Hello?" She mumbled into her phone at 9 o'clock the morning after the ball.

"OH MY GOD! YOU'RE TRENDING ON TWITTER!!" Fern shrieked joyously at the other end.

"Huh?" Elise rolled over and blinked blearily at the clock.

"I said you're trending on Twitter!" She sounded so ridiculously excited it took a couple of seconds for Elise to register what she'd said.

"I'm trending on Twitter?" she repeated dully and Fern sighed.

"Well kind of. Not you but it's about you. Is your computer on?"

Elise closed her eyes and lay back on the pillow. "I didn't get home until almost 4am, Fern. No, my computer is not on."

"Damn, did I wake you up?" At least she sounded contrite.

"Yeah, but it's okay. You can tell me about it."

"Everyone's guessing who Mr X is. There are pictures of you and Taylor all over the news this morning and they think it might be him."

"Fuck." Elise dragged a pillow over her head. "We made the news?"

"Yeah, you did." She sounded massively amused.

"I'd better call Nate."

For the first time Fern's excitement dulled. "He won't be angry will he?"

"I shouldn't think so. He knows we're just friends. But it might come as a nasty shock to him to see pictures of me in the papers."

"If it's any consolation, you looked absolutely gorgeous. That dress was stunning."

"I should bloody hope so considering it probably costs more than my monthly salary," Elise grumbled, making a mental note to look up how much a one-off Roberto Cavalli gown went for.

"I saw a similar one on the net for just over two grand." Fern admitted sheepishly. "I looked it up."

"Well add in the shoes and accessories and you probably have my annual salary, let alone my monthly one." Elise slumped. "This is going to be a nightmare isn't it? What are the papers saying?"

"They're speculating that you and Taylor are an item, that he's Mr X and that you're the reason he and his brother had a bust up. Did he really break his brother's nose?"

"Yeah." She pounded a pillow in frustration. "Yes he did."

"Can I come visit?" Fern started to laugh. "Your life is like a soap opera."

"You're welcome any time, but don't expect any drama. And could you please be a little less amused by all this?" Elise knew she sounded grumpy but Fern obviously didn't realise what a big deal this was. "Taylor is a big man in the city. I'm a nobody. This could damage his reputation."

"You're hardly a nobody!" she protested. "You're a published author with a blog that more than two hundred thousand people follow."

"What?" Elise was floored. She knew a lot of the magazine readers checked her blog out but she didn't realise it was that many.

"Look, I'll let you get back to sleep, but if I was you I'd turn the phone off and when you get up you should check your computer, okay?"

"Okay. Bye." Elise ended the call, sent Nathan a text message telling him to just come over whenever because she was turning her phone off, switched the phone off and promptly went back to sleep.

She was woken just before midday by the buzzer and answered it in her pyjamas. "Yo."

"Wow, someone sounds like they have a sore head this morning." Nathan sounded cheerful which was good.

"No, I just woke up." She pushed the button to let him into the building and slouched through to the kitchen to put the kettle on while she waited for him to come up.

"I'm surprised there aren't any reporters out there." He commented as he came through the door, taking over the coffee making from her so she could sit down.

"They probably don't know where I live. I haven't seen the news. Is it bad?"

He made a so-so gesture. "It's not bad but everyone is talking about it. Why don't you go get in the shower and I'll make you some lunch? You can't go to dance class looking like that."

"I think you're the best boyfriend ever." She kissed him and went to the bathroom to do as suggested.

When she returned Nathan had the television on and the news was just going to the local segment. To her horror there was a picture of her and Taylor on the dance floor as the third headline in and she watched aghast as the news reader broke out in a grin.

"Of course the talk in the city this morning is all about this romantic love story. Are Taylor Stone and Elise Waterford an item? And who is the mysterious Mr X? We go now to our entertainment reporter Blake Chisholm."

"Thank you Tamara. Last night at the benefit ball to raise money for the crisis in Sudan, many eyebrows were raised when Taylor Stone, millionaire playboy and editor of Monochrome Magazine, turned up with a mysterious brunette on his arm." The screen cut to video of the two of them working the red carpet and Elise could only be grateful that she didn't look anywhere near as dazed as she had felt. *"Inside sources revealed that the woman is Elise*

Waterford, who joined the magazine a few weeks ago and is currently writing a hit blog for the magazine on internet dating. There have been rumours for weeks that Taylor Stone was no longer an eligible bachelor, fuelled by his distinct lack of womanising recently and further fuelled by an argument between he and his brother, Anton Stone. Anton is rumoured to have told close friends and associates that he disapproves of his brother's relationship with Elise Waterford. Both of the brothers and their father, media mogul George Stone, have been unavailable for comment this morning."

"And Blake, what can you tell us about Mr X? It seems to be a love story that has gripped the city." Well there was an exaggeration if ever Elise had heard one. Gripped the city? She snorted. Hardly.

"Well, Tamara, since Ms Waterford started blogging on the magazine's website, an anonymous person known only as Mr X has been leaving love letters in the comments section for her. Ms Waterford has not yet commented in her blog towards Mr X, but it is widely speculated that Mr X is an acquaintance of hers. Sources close to Ms Waterford say she has no idea who he is."

"What sources?" Elise was confused. "Who have they been speaking to? I don't know anyone here except for you and your friends."

Nathan looked angry. "It'll have been leaked from the magazine. This is good publicity for them."

"Is there a possibility that Mr X is Taylor Stone?" The female newsreader was asking and the reporter shrugged.

"Nobody knows for sure, but witnesses say they looked pretty happy last night. It's not out of the realms of possibility. Of course there are other contenders for the title of Mr X. Her first subject for the feature, a man known only as Mark, may be responsible for the postings. It has even

been speculated that Mr X may be Anton Stone and that this was the cause of the row between he and Taylor."

"I can't watch any more of this." Elise turned away. "Switch it off."

Nathan pressed the button and the screen went blank. "It'll blow over in a couple of days." He tried to reassure her. "There's no blog post now until Monday. In two days there'll be plenty of other news to fill the gap."

"I hope so." But Elise was troubled. She had a bad feeling about this and knew that it could only get worse.

After a quiet lunch of soup and sandwiches they headed across town to the dance studio and spent an enjoyable couple of hours practicing their tango. They were actually getting pretty good for novices and the sheer pleasure of it distracted Elise enough from the mess of her social life that she was able to relax for the first time that day.

It lasted until they got out of the studio and her phone beeped with a voicemail from Taylor.

"Elise, I'm guessing by now you've seen the news." He sounded tired. "I suggest you keep your head down for a couple of days. Nobody knows where you live so, as long as no-one gets the chance to follow you, you should be fine. I've got reporters camped outside my door otherwise I'd be there. We've had some requests coming into the office and we'll deal with them for the moment but I strongly advise you to get an agent. I'm sending you an email with the number of a company we use. I've given them a heads up that they'll hear from you. I'll try and call you again later." There was a brief pause. "Sorry." He hung up.

"Taylor says I need to lay low for a couple of days." She told Nathan as they walked.

"That's probably a good idea. I'll go shopping for you." He shrugged easily and Elise stared at him.

"I can't believe you're taking this so well." She said and he shrugged again.

"Don't get me wrong, I'm pretty raging. I think Taylor set it up this way – his family own a media empire...he had to know that taking you to the ball would fuel the rumours. But it's done and there's nothing we can do about it now. Shouting a lot and pointing fingers isn't going to help or fix anything. Right now the best thing to do is follow his advice and try and minimise the amount of disruption to your life as possible and hope that this goes away."

"Do you think I should go back to Scotland?" She asked, worried, and he shook his head.

"No. Your home there is a matter of public record. Down here your name isn't attached in any way to the apartment or, in fact, to me so unless someone at the magazine spills the beans again there's no way they can find you." He frowned. "Unless the magazine decides it's too good a story and try to milk it in which case they might let slip."

"I think I can trust them." Elise was still in too much shock to think straight but she was just getting comfortable in her flat and didn't want to disrupt all that again.

"Fine, but if you change your mind it's the work of seconds to pack you a bag. You can stay at mine." They descended into the tube station and, wary of people looking at her, she tucked her face into his chest as they waited for a train. This was just a nightmare.

To: Elise Waterford
(elise.waterford@monochrome.co.uk)
From: Mr X (X_Towers@hotmail.com)

Elise,
I saw you on the news this morning. You looked absolutely gorgeous at the ball. That dress was spectacular. Try and ignore the media hounds, they'll forget about it soon enough when some other story comes along.
Ever yours,
X

To: Mr X (X_Towers@hotmail.com)
From: Elise Waterford
(elise.waterford@monochrome.co.uk)

X,
Don't try to compliment or reassure me. I'm mad at you.
Elise

To: Elise Waterford
(elise.waterford@monochrome.co.uk)
From: Mr X (X_Towers@hotmail.com)

Elise,
Why are you mad at me? I can't help that the media have blown this all totally out of proportion.
Ever yours,
X

To: Mr X (X_Towers@hotmail.com)
From: Elise Waterford
(elise.waterford@monochrome.co.uk)

X,
Don't try and reason with me. I'm tired and upset and I've run out of chocolate. I'm entitled to be irrational.
Elise

To: Elise Waterford
(elise.waterford@monochrome.co.uk)
From: Mr X (X_Towers@hotmail.com)

Elise,
YOU'VE RUN OUT OF CHOCOLATE?! *horrified* This is indeed a sad state of affairs.
Ever yours,

X

To: Mr X (X_Towers@hotmail.com)
From: Elise Waterford
(elise.waterford@monochrome.co.uk)

X,
Tell me about it.
Elise

On Saturday evening Harry came over and Elise cooked them Mexican before they watched a film together. He didn't say whether he'd seen the news or not and they didn't bring it up. It was nice to have a slice of normality, even if it was only for a few hours. On Sunday they decided to bake and attempted a Baked Alaska. Nathan couldn't decide if he liked it more than the chocolate and beetroot cake and declared it joint favourite. At least until the next time they baked at which point, no doubt, he would declare whatever they were baking as his new favourite.

When Elise sat in front of her computer on Monday morning, her inbox was full and she put the radio on as she began flicking through them. A lot were spam but there were several from family members saying they'd seen her on the news and a few from various friends. There was another email from Mr X, from Sunday afternoon, to say he hoped she was okay with the media circus going on and would be there if she needed someone to freak out to. There were a couple from Taylor that she kept for last because she didn't think she could face them at that time on a Monday morning, but the one that really shook her was a summons from George Stone, Taylor's father, requesting her presence at the office on Thursday. She sent a brief reply saying she'd be there at four o'clock and blind copied it to Taylor, hoping he'd have some idea what it was about. Taylor's first email contained the details of the agency he had promised and Elise called them quickly, leaving her name and number for someone to get back to her. They assured her they already had it in hand and would be in touch when they had a digest of offers for her to peruse. She didn't ask what offers she had received – she wasn't interested in being paraded as a possible plus one of Taylor's. His second email was a personal one, telling her he'd had a lovely time at the ball and was sorry about the fall-out from it. He asked how she was getting on with the projects and reminded her that she was halfway through the hardest part. He signed off with warmest wishes and Elise sighed. It would be rude not to reply to it so she answered all his questions, stated she too had a lovely time at the ball and brushed off the consequent media storm politely. There wasn't much else she could say.

When that was done, she still didn't feel like working, so she logged onto the internet just as the news was starting. To her horror they were still speculating about her relationship with Taylor. He had been absent from the city's clubs all weekend and the Magazine was officially keeping quiet on all fronts regarding any rumours. The continued silence was sending the reporters into a frenzy, like a shoal of piranhas. To make matters worse, a couple of people in high society had openly said they didn't believe that Taylor was Mr X for exactly the same reason Elise didn't. He just didn't seem the romantic type. It wasn't his style. As a result the reporters were speculating wildly on who it might be. A 'Mr X Rumours' hash tag had started up on Twitter where people could exchange guesses, each wilder and crazier than the last. It was a disaster.

When she'd heard enough she switched the radio off and logged into the blog. She hadn't read any of the comments left by Mr X the week before but she'd heard snippets in the news casts and realised she was woefully ill-prepared to answer any questions put to her about them.

At least if she read them she'd have some idea what she was dealing with.

Monday – Elise, You need never be afraid my love. You bring out the best in people just by being you...a fiercely beautiful, humble and wonderful woman. Go fearlessly, be brave, be reckless...have faith. There is nothing you cannot overcome or achieve if you just believed in yourself as much as I believe in you. Ever yours...

Wednesday – Elise, My heart hurts to hear that you have suffered so. You seem so strong, so full of heart and larger than life, that it is almost impossible to imagine that you were ever vulnerable. Any man on a journey such as that you are undertaking with Jim would be lucky to have you at his side. I'm sure you had friends and people to hold your hand on your journey into the darkness. At this time remember how that felt and know that Jim will be as grateful to you as you were to them. And you are not alone. You still have your friends...you still have me. You will get through this and be a brighter and more glorious star in the tenements of beauty than you are now because of it. Ever yours...

Friday – Elise, Firstly I am so proud of you for being strong enough to take Jim on this journey. He is a lucky man. Secondly, it is not just those to whom we confess our love that can be broken by the saying or not saying of those three words. It breaks me a little more every day that I cannot tell you I love you, that I must say it silently within my heart. It is an agony of inconstancy, my heart at war with my head. Finally, the good of men often lives long after they have gone. If ever you fear that your deeds are forgotten remember your histories...people that fought and died for love, those that gave selflessly of themselves to better mankind. Think Florence Nightingale, Mother Theresa, Mahatma Ghandi, Martin Luther King Jr...sure, there may have been a few negative things about them, but they are remembered for the good they did in this world. Don't ever fear that the kindnesses you do each day will not live on...I think you underestimate the impact you have on people's lives. You cannot say how many children will be born into this world as a result of your attempts to enrich these mens' lives with love. Those are your legacy, spoken or unspoken. If you walk in the light of all that is right and good in this world then when you move on you will have left a little ray of sunshine in the souls of all those who came into contact with you. Ever yours...

Elise blinked and read that last again. Clearly an educated and well read man then. She didn't know anyone that would use the word 'inconstancy' in common parlance and she couldn't remember off-hand ever seeing a writing style similar to his amongst her friends. He had given something away though...he was clearly a person she had not been in contact with during the three years before and immediately after her move to Scotland. She'd been too emotional on Wednesday night to pick up on that. That narrowed it down considerably to people she had been at school or university with or someone she had met either in her village back home or someone she had met in London. It neatly checked off all her closest friends, most of whom had been aware of the counselling and the preceding events. It wasn't much but it was somewhere to start.

When she couldn't procrastinate any more she picked up the file for project four and settled down to read.

Chapter 11

There's something to be said for a revelation that occurs during the eating of a marmalade sandwich. That something is that you can't screech "Holy Moly Batman!" without spraying the person opposite you with partially masticated goodness. Thus forced to keep one's mouth shut, one avoids having to explain one's thought process to the unfortunate sprayee. This minimises any need to contact the men in white coats. Today's epiphany was this - I am a life with chunks kind of girl. I've never really understood the point of shredless marmalade or smooth peanut butter. I don't buy orange juice without bits and I can't understand why anyone would eat dairy milk when they can have Toblerone with all its chewy goodness. Why buy white bread when you can buy whole grain with all those flies and bits of cardboard and extra protein swept up from the bakery floor?

There are unspoken food rules to that effect in my house, but up until the reading of Project 4's profile today I had never extrapolated this rule to the rest of my life. There is very little in my life that does, or in fact has, run smoothly. Not for me are the clockwork days, the tidy house, the perfect relationships. Sometimes I fear that I can't do anything in a sane or normal fashion but, after a whole two seconds of freaking out, I shrug and get on with it. My bumpy life, full of crunchy bits and whole grains and citrus shreds, has led me to become a genius of adaptation, disingenuousness and divertive distraction. On an emotional level, I think this way of life has led me to be one of the strongest people I know. My sheer inability to get anything right without at least three or four hiccups along the way has led me to an understanding that a life along a bumpy road is actually a blessing in disguise.

But more obviously it applies to my taste in men. Every girl has a guy she crushes on that she probably shouldn't admit to, right? For me it's Robert Downey Jr. He has made so many screw-ups in his life that I find him fascinating. I'm not into the pretty boys and the vacant stares, the glossy lives and the assorted adopted children. I have issues with Brad Pitt's nostrils. I'm into people with a story to tell and a depth that only a 'life with bits' can give you. Until you have walked in the darkness, you will never understand the value of the light. I need a man that will turn me on intellectually as well as physically, a mirror for the darkness in my own soul that provides a backdrop for all the joy in my life. When it comes to the Vampire Diaries I am aaaalllll about Damon... I know what I like, even when I know it's not necessarily good for me.

Project four is a man called Simon. Simon is all about what he doesn't want. His profile is a list of the things he dislikes and doesn't want in a woman and reading it all makes me wonder if he knows what he actually <u>does</u> like. It feels like he's so focused on the negative that I don't think he's ever actually stopped to consider the positive. He hasn't even put anything about himself in his profile so I have no idea at all what kind of a man I'm dealing with.

I have no idea what tomorrow will bring.

As she always did after writing her blog post, she checked her email and ignored all the ones from various relatives and friends, looking for the ones from Mr X. Finally she found one, sent that morning.

To: Elise Waterford (<u>elise.waterford@monochrome.co.uk</u>) From: Mr X (<u>X_Towers@hotmail.com</u>)

Elise,
Good luck this week. I'm praying for you that it's easier than last week and that all this crazy media circus that's going on doesn't put too much pressure on you. Wish I could give you a hug. This must seem like the worst kind of hell for you. Let me know how you get on.
Ever yours,
X

Weird that his email should make her feel instantly better. She'd come to look forward to his missives, even though she still felt a little uncomfortable about his comments on her blog. It frustrated the hell out of her that she couldn't work out who he was. She accepted that he was an acquaintance of hers, someone she did actually know, but beyond that it was a mystery. She knew it was wrong to have flirted with him while she was dating Nate but there was something refreshingly honest about an email conversation that you just didn't get face to face.

To: Mr X (X_Towers@hotmail.com)
From: Elise Waterford
(elise.waterford@monochrome.co.uk)

X,
I'm ok. A little freaked out by everything that's going on but I'm just keeping my head down and trying to get on with life. What about you? Must be weird to have everyone wondering about your identity.
Elise

To: Elise Waterford
(elise.waterford@monochrome.co.uk)
From: Mr X (X_Towers@hotmail.com)

Elise,

Yeah, it is a little weird isn't it? Mostly I'm ignoring it. I can't really complain since it was me that started it in the first place by leaving you love letters. I have been watching the rumours hashtag on twitter though. Some of the suggestions have been very amusing. I never expected it to get so...big. Makes it worse in a way because there'll be so much interest if I reveal myself.
Ever yours,
X

To: Mr X (X_Towers@hotmail.com)
From: Elise Waterford
(elise.waterford@monochrome.co.uk)

X,
I wish you would reveal yourself. I look forward to your emails. It would be nice to know who I'm corresponding with.
Elise

To: Elise Waterford
(elise.waterford@monochrome.co.uk)
From: Mr X (X_Towers@hotmail.com)

Elise,
You're corresponding with someone that cares for you very deeply. I've thought a lot recently about telling you who I am but I'm aware that you're dating someone. That being the case, I'm going to keep my silence. I don't want to put you in the position of having to choose unless you're unhappy and looking for a way out.
Ever yours,
X

To: Mr X (X_Towers@hotmail.com)
From: Elise Waterford
(elise.waterford@monochrome.co.uk)

X,
I'm not unhappy. He's a great guy. I appreciate the
sentiment though.
Elise

To: Elise Waterford
(elise.waterford@monochrome.co.uk)
From: Mr X (X_Towers@hotmail.com)

Elise,
And yet you still email and flirt with me?
Ever yours,
X

To: Mr X (X_Towers@hotmail.com)
From: Elise Waterford
(elise.waterford@monochrome.co.uk)

X,
Are we flirting? I told you I wasn't perfect.
Elise

To: Elise Waterford
(elise.waterford@monochrome.co.uk)
From: Mr X (X_Towers@hotmail.com)

Elise,
Yes we are. And think about it. If you were 100%
happy with him you wouldn't have emailed me back in the
first place. Curiosity is the first step on the path to
insecurity.
Ever yours,
X

Elise stared at the screen, unsure whether to feel
angry, affronted or freaked out. True, Nate could be a little

smothering and over-protective. He might be jealous and a little insecure when it came to other men. He might constantly turn up unannounced to spend time with her, but they loved each other and were still in the first flushes of their relationship. Surely that intensity was normal, right? Damn Mr X for putting doubts in her mind. Who was he to question when he couldn't even be bothered to tell her who he was? Angry, she slammed the lid of the laptop down and went to bake a cake.

On Tuesday morning Elise followed her usual pattern of meeting her project at a cafe. Simon turned out to be an average guy. Average height, average build, average looks... His attitude was pretty average too. She had been spot on about his total inability to decide what he wanted in a woman. He was so cut up about a multitude of previous failed relationships that, instead of looking forward, he was maintaining a list of the least desirable traits of his ex-girlfriends in his mind and judging everyone against it. Elise didn't know where to start. She didn't think counselling would help in this case. What she needed to do was find out what he liked and she had no idea how to go about that.

She spent the afternoon pacing around the flat feeling like a caged animal at the zoo. She wanted to go do stuff but Taylor's warnings about keeping her head down were making her feel like she couldn't even step outside the front door. She was still too angry with X to turn on her computer and check her emails. When Nathan arrived to take her to dance class she was so relieved she thought she might cry.

She threw everything she had into dancing and by the time they made it home and ate takeaway she was so exhausted she didn't know what to do with herself.

"Why don't I run you a bath?" Nathan suggested, stroking her back soothingly as she leaned up against him in the kitchen. "You look beat."

"That sounds great." She told him dully.

"Don't get too enthusiastic..." He joked but it fell flat and concern clouded his face. "Is it the rumours or is it the feature?" He asked and she sighed.

"A little of both." She admitted. "I have no idea where I'm going with project 4. I can't tell someone what to love. How do you find out what type you like in less than a week? Isn't it trial and error?"

"I guess." He thought about it. "I didn't know really what my type was until I met you. I thought I was into geek chic but you're kinda normal."

"Gee, thanks!" She chuckled, her mood lightening slightly. "Perhaps that's it. He must have fallen for his ex girlfriends for some reason. I need to find out what he saw in them from before they broke his heart."

"That's going to be a fun conversation." He remarked drily, resting his cheek against her head. "I don't envy you at all.

"Well, it certainly can't be as hard as last week." Elise said quietly, sadness clouding her tone. "That was painful."

"You know, if you want to quit this project I'm behind you all the way." He told her quietly, stroking her hair.

"If I quit I have to go back to Scotland," she pointed out and he sighed.

"No. You wouldn't. You'll come and live with me."

"I need to work, Nathan," she grumbled. "I have bills to pay."

"I know. But as long as you know it's an option..." Leaving her to think about it, he went to run the bath.

I've never really had a type. In fairness, when it comes to men I don't really ask for much. They have to be employed, not have a criminal record and be a non-smoker. I couldn't date a smoker. It's like licking a dirty ashtray. Obviously that's not the total list. I have to find them attractive on some level. I've never really had a physical type, although I guess I tend to go for guys that are taller than me. I guess what I'm trying to say is that I've never really looked objectively at potential partners in terms of what they look like. I've also never specifically gone out looking for a certain kind of guy. I guess you could say I'm an equal opportunities prospector.

The point is, I don't suppose many of us have actually thought about what we want as opposed to what we don't want. I don't suppose many of us have even really thought about what we don't want full stop. I suspect it's an issue fairly unique to Simon and it's a habit I need to break him of. The problem is that I need to force him to think about what he wants, because trying to get him to back off from his negativity on the basis of a nebulous attempt to not judge at all will be too difficult.

This is going to be an awkward conversation to have. When you leave someone, it's easy to remember the bad things about them but painful to remember the good things about them...why you fell for them in the first place. I think it must also hurt to look for people based on things you found attractive in other women. It's a fine line to walk to ensure you don't get reminded of your ex-partners whenever you look at your new girlfriend.

The other potential pitfall here is what happens if what he looks for in woman is either grossly chauvinistic or totally unattainable. Perhaps all his previous girlfriends have been six-foot tall leggy blondes with pneumatic chests, MENSA quality IQ and a physique based on Barbie. And how on earth do you put that on a profile? "Dudes, I'm looking for Dr Barbie..." I can't see he'd get many takers.

I suppose only time will tell – we'll have this conversation tomorrow and then attempt to rewrite his profile.

On Thursday morning Elise was woken up at 8am by Fern on the phone again.

"S'up?" She mumbled and Fern whooped excitedly.

"You're trending again!" She squeaked. "You lucky thing you! This Nathan sounds like a real catch! Have you seen the news? Fuck, I woke you up again didn't I?"

"What are you talking about?"

Fern instantly sobered. "Go watch the news." She said. "It's all over the breakfast shows." Without saying anything else she hung up and Elise sighed, resigned to yet another early morning.

"Who was that?" Nathan asked coming back from the bathroom.

"Fern. Apparently I'm trending again and I'm on the news."

"You going to get up?" He asked cautiously and she sighed again.

"I guess I probably should." Wearily she dragged herself out of bed and slouched through to the living room, flicking through the channels as Nathan went to put the coffee on. Stopping when she caught a glimpse of her name she stopped and watched.

"This week we've been reporting on the love story of Elise Waterford, star blogger for Monochrome Magazine." Declared the presenter. *"It has become something of a cult phenomenon in the city and since yesterday a Spartacus-type campaign has hit the city streets in a rash of T-shirts with the moniker '#IamMrX'."*

The screen cut to pictures of men on the tube and in the streets wearing the T-shirts. That was bearable. In a way Elise could even see the humour of it, but her grin faded when the screen cut back to the presenter.

"In an interesting twist to the Mr X story, Elise Waterford has now been linked to Nathan Redwood,

favourite grandson of billionaire business tycoon Elias Redwood. Nathan and his brother Harry are set to inherit trust funds of up to 48 million pounds each when they reach their 30th birthdays." The presenter grinned. "She sure can choose these guys."

The blood drained from her face and she heard Nathan swearing quietly behind her.

"Is this true?" She whispered, turning panicked eyes towards him. "I don't understand. I thought you were a librarian. Are you really a millionaire?"

"It's not that simple." He looked anguished. "Elise I can't stay, I've got to go to work. Can we talk about this tonight?"

"Answer me one thing?" She looked so pale that he didn't have the heart to say no.

"What is it?"

"Why did you tell me that Taylor had so much more? Do you love me?"

"Of course I love you!" He rushed across and hugged her fiercely. "I love you so much it hurts. As for Taylor...I'll have to explain that later. It's tied into the money. I promise you we'll talk about it. I'll come straight here from work."

"Okay." He kissed her cheek and rushed out the door so he wouldn't be late. Still in shock and feeling slightly dazed, Elise showered and dressed and went to meet Simon.

A painful and long four hours later she had a workable list and set off home to start writing her profile and Friday's blog post. She saw a few of the T-shirts on her journey to his house and back but after the bomb shell of that morning they didn't seem so amusing. She sat in front of the computer for almost an hour, just staring at the screen, but she couldn't seem to focus. The words just wouldn't come. Finally she gave up and logged into the blog. She hadn't looked at Mr X's posts since the previous week and had blogged twice since then.

Monday – *Elise, if there is darkness in your soul I consider it to be the velvet glory of the night sky, a shimmering and glorious backdrop for the fiery brilliance of the stars. Ever yours...in darkness and in joy.*

Wednesday – *Elise, one of the things I love most about you is that you never seem judge people. You're not just equal opportunities when it comes to prospective partners – you give everyone you come into contact with a free pass to walk right into your heart. It's a generous, selfless and utterly endearing way to live. It makes me wonder...if you knew who I was would you judge me? Ever yours...*

Well...he certainly had a way with words. Night sky indeed. Elise sighed and closed the browser window just as the phone rang.

Fern didn't even wait for her to reply. "OH MY GOD!" She shrieked, beside herself with excitement. "YOU'RE TRENDING GLOBALLY!!"

"Why now?" She knew why. It was to do with Nathan. She just wanted to hear it from someone else.

"Apparently this Nate you've been dating is a billionsquillionaire." Fern paused. "Pretty dishy too from the pictures that have been posted. There's also some sort of movement to set you up on a blind date with Mr X. You should go check it out."

"I will." Elise facepalmed. The only way this could go was down Embarrassment Terrace which led onto Mortification Avenue which ended in the cul-de-sac of Ground Please Open and Swallow Me Whole. "Do you spend your whole day on Twitter? How come you know all this stuff?"

"Well I check it every now and then, but I always look at your page first because it's far more interesting than mine. I still have your password from when I set it up for you."

"Oh. I see." Shaking her head, Elise had to smile. She was glad someone was delighted with the turn of events. "I'll check it out and text you later, I promise. I've got to work now."

"Okay. I just thought you should know."

"Love you." Elise hung up and stared at the computer. It was going to be a long afternoon.

She was just contemplating the merits of coffee when her phone rang again. This time it was Mark.

"Are you busy this afternoon?" He asked once they'd been through the small talk. "I have something I'd like to show you."

Elise thought about the blog and the profile. "No." She lied. "I've got an appointment at four, but other than that I'm not busy. You want me to come over?"

"I'm at the gallery hanging pictures. Can you come here instead?"

"Sure." Elise grabbed a piece of paper to write down the address, took her tube map and headed out into the sunshine. It was a swelteringly hot day and by the time she arrived at the gallery her hair was a frazzled mess and her T-shirt was sticking to her damp skin. Mark hugged her warmly anyway as he met her at the door and led her through into a huge, airy and bright space.

"So you got a gallery exhibition?" She queried. It was kind of obvious given that his photos were hanging up everywhere but she wanted to hear it from the beginning.

"Yeah the studio has been negotiating for a while but it was your photographs that clinched the deal."

"My photographs?" Elise's heart sank.

"Come with me." He took her hand and led her through to another brightly lit room where the only photos were a series of pictures all along the far wall. They were so beautiful that it took a moment for Elise to realise she was looking at herself.

"Oh my God!" She stared at them. "That's me!"

"Yes." He seemed amused. "We called it Kaleidoscope." He gestured to the tiny plaques beneath each picture, each with an emotion printed on it – happiness, sorrow, worry... "Your face is so expressive. In half an hour I managed to capture a whole cycle of these from joy through everything else and back to joy again. The gallery loved it."

She felt a bit self-conscious about the whole thing but the pictures really were beautiful. "You'll let me know if anyone buys one?" She asked and he nodded.

"Of course."

She wandered around looking at the rest of the photographs and spent a few moments catching up on the gossip with Mark. One of his dates had been really successful and it was looking like she might be the one. He was elated and she left the gallery with a bounce in her step. It was hard not to be utterly delighted for him.

She didn't have enough time to go home before her appointment at the office so she just headed straight there. She didn't know what Mr Stone wanted to see her for but if he wasn't happy with her wearing jeans he could go whistle. He might own the magazine, but Taylor had employed her and he was her manager. If Nathan was right and the magazine knew exactly what they were doing floating the rumours about Taylor after the ball, then she owed them nothing for making her life awkward.

As expected, he made her wait almost half an hour before she was called through to the office. When she finally went through she had to hide a smile. George Stone was almost exactly what she had imagined – an older, more rugged version of Taylor. The beautiful bone structure and blond hair were there, just slightly more weathered by time.

"Miss Waterford," he greeted. "Take a seat."

"Thanks." Refusing to be intimidated by the expanse of desk between them, she settled herself comfortably in a chair and focused on him. "What can I do for you?"

He didn't waste any time on small talk. "Miss Waterford, I want to know what your intentions are towards my son."

"Taylor?" Elise shrugged. "We're just friends. We've only ever been and will only ever be friends. I have a partner."

"Have you made that clear to my son?"

Irritated now, Elise levelled him a steady gaze. "I wasn't aware it was in my contract to nursemaid your son when it comes to explaining the obvious."

For the first time he cracked a smile. "Touché, Miss Waterford. Nice to see you have some fire in you. No doubt you are aware by now that this has the potential to become a media storm?"

She shrugged helplessly. "This is all new to me. I can't understand why anyone would be interested in me."

"It's a fairytale of the finest order." He leaned back in his chair. "You, the penniless girl from nowhere, and my son...the obscenely wealthy Prince Charming. It's a Cinderella Story. Of course the public is fascinated by it. Thousands of girls cry themselves to sleep every night wishing they were you."

There was nothing she could say to that. She couldn't even argue his point despite her irritation at being described as a penniless nobody. "So what are *your* intentions?" she asked eventually and he steepled his fingers, resting his chin on them.

"If I ordered you to stop seeing my son, would you?"

"No." She stared him down defiantly. "Who my friends are is not your decision to make. And if you had any respect for your son, you'd realise that it's not your business who *his* friends are. He's old enough and ugly enough to make his own decisions."

"Ordinarily yes, but love makes fools of us all, Miss Waterford. I only want to protect my son and from what Anton tells me, Taylor is clearly in love with you."

"Then shouldn't you be speaking to Taylor about that?" she suggested drily. "He knows I'm with someone else. I can't tell him how to feel. Besides, isn't this all great publicity for the magazine? Two or three months down the line everyone will have forgotten about this, but you'll have made millions."

"How very mercenary of you." Amusement was evident in his tone. "I have to say, I admire your balls. It's unfortunate that Taylor wants you. You'd be an interesting asset to the company."

"I *am* an interesting asset to the company," she pointed out. "Since I started blogging, traffic to the site has increased by more than tenfold." She left unsaid that getting rid of her would damage the magazine's ratings, but he understood. She could almost see the cogs turning behind his shrewd eyes.

"You will come to dinner with us this Sunday," he announced abruptly and she stared at him, trying to figure out where he was going with this.

"I have plans," she told him shortly. "My boyfriend's family invited me for Sunday lunch." It had been more of an open invitation than a specific one, but this week they'd just have to go.

"Then Saturday should be fine."

"I have a class I can't miss on Saturday evening," she shot right back and there was a brief flicker of amusement in his eyes.

"When can you come for dinner, Miss Waterford?"

"When I am invited without an ulterior motive. I will not be used as a pawn in your publicity game, Mr Stone."

He sighed. "I can see why my son likes you." He gave a twisted grin. "It's rather refreshing to be put in my place. Very well. I will leave you alone. Just do not harm my son."

"I won't." She got to her feet and walked to the door, but before she got there she paused and turned back to him. "Tell him my resignation will be on his desk on Monday morning." Without giving him a chance to respond, she slipped out of the door and walked unsteadily towards the lifts. She didn't know if she'd just made a massive mistake, but this wasn't her life. She didn't want to be involved in power games between London's financial players. She felt a sudden yearning to be home in her own bed in Scotland and it ached so fiercely it was like the oxygen had been sucked out of her lungs.

She was barely out of the building when her mobile began ringing. Checking the display she saw it was Taylor and sent the call to voicemail and set the phone to silent. She didn't need to speak to him right now, she was so torn between anger and sadness. He could wait for another day, preferably when she was packed and on a flight back to Scotland.

When she got back to the apartment, Nathan was waiting in the hall. She hadn't given him a key so he was sat against the door with a bag of shopping that looked like the makings of dinner.

"Sorry." She helped him up. "I had a meeting at the office." She took a deep breath. "I resigned."

"You what?" Realising she was upset, he dropped the bag of shopping and gathered her in a hug. "Oh, honey, I'm sorry. I know you were enjoying the job."

"It wasn't worth it." Before she realised it, her face was wet and her shoulders were shaking.

"Come on," he said gently, steering her towards the door. "Let's get the kettle on and you can tell me all about it."

As he made dinner, she relayed the conversation with George Stone and he frowned. "What an ass. You're right...resigning was the right thing to do. They need you more than you need them, so maybe they'll learn a lesson. Who knows?"

"But I don't know what to do now, Nathan." She'd stopped crying but she was still miserable. "You still haven't explained all that stuff on the news this morning. I don't know if I should stay here or just get the first flight back to Scotland. I'm so angry with you. I feel like I've been lied to non-stop and I'm so homesick for my cottage."

He looked stricken. "Please stay!" He ran his hands through his hair. "Look, my grandfather is a very wealthy man. It's true. It's also true that I'm his favourite and that Harry and I both have trust funds, but there were conditions attached to those trust funds. He wanted us to understand the value of money. Like my father before us he insisted that we live the first 30 years of our lives as normal people in normal size houses with normal jobs and normal financial worries. There were no bail-outs, no loans...nothing. I've spent my fair share of nights lying awake worrying about how I'm going to pay bills. It's a good lesson to learn. You've been to my mum and dad's house. Did you think they were rich when you met them?"

She shook her head. "No, they just seemed like regular people."

"My dad has more money than Harry and I combined will." He explained. "But he knows what it means. He invests it, he gives a lot to charity and they live a comfortable life but he spent 3 decades learning the lesson that it shouldn't be frittered away on pointless things. If you become too spoilt to deal with it responsibly then you're wasting the decent things you could do with it. You see all these spoilt little rich kids crashing and burning on drugs and alcohol and for what? What have they achieved with their lives? The money isn't going to change me. I'll be the same guy, probably in the same house and maybe even with the same job...I'll just never have to lie awake at night worrying anymore."

"I get that. I really do." Elise nodded. "What I don't understand is why you thought Taylor has more? I mean...the minute you start getting into six figures it doesn't really matter what the number starts with."

"It's not about the money. It's about the lifestyle." He frowned as he tried to think how to explain it. "Taylor grew up in different circles to me. He knows people. He moves among the rich and famous. There is nothing that man couldn't give you with a few words in the right ears and that's not something I can do for you. I can't give you all your dreams on a platter in the way that he could."

"And is that still what you think?"

"No." He came around the worktop and gathered her in his arms. "I think that if you have the kind of dreams that are all about money and connections then I haven't learned the lesson my grandpa is trying to teach me."

"I can't believe you ever thought me shallow enough to be concerned by it." She didn't hug him back, shaking her head. "I'm so confused Nathan. Do you mind if I stay on my own tonight?"

"No it's okay. I understand." Slightly subdued he let her go and they ate their dinner in near silence.

This will be my final blog for this magazine. Simon has his profile and he's ready to start dating. I think he learned some important lessons about love...that sometimes you have to look for the best in people and remember them that way. It's like when someone you love dies. You see them in the hospital and for the longest time that's how you remember them – pale, frail and wasted. But over time you remember other things...the memories you shared, all the love and the laughter. After a while those memories don't even hurt anymore and you start to feel a little joy in them. When that's happened it's time to let go and move on and soon you'll wake up one day and realise that you haven't thought about them for a while. For a couple of hours you'll be scared and shaken and then, slowly, you'll accept it and life will move you on once again. Sure, you'll cry every now and then when their favourite song comes on the radio or on a particularly poignant anniversary, but that sorrow will be tempered with joy and if you're really lucky you'll spend some time realising how knowing them made you a better and stronger person. That was the lesson Simon needed to learn and I think he's on the first few steps there.

I too have learned a lot about love on this journey. I came into this project with this naive idea that internet dating was all about a formula, that finding love was almost like following a recipe, but it's not. Looking for love is a profound and life-changing experience in which being honest is the bottom line. You have to be honest with yourself, honest with the people around you. And being honest with yourself is a brutal process. Sometimes being realistic about yourself is a question of raising your self-esteem, not lowering it. You have to believe that you are worthy of love and when you've spent years believing yourself worthless, with society reinforcing that, it's almost impossible to achieve. You have to be honest about your hopes and dreams, the things that mean the most to you.

Loving is about honesty and being brave enough to accept the truth. Love is about having fears and sharing and facing them together. Love is about learning who we are, where we came from and how we came to be the people we are today. Love is amazing and complex and anyone who has found it is both honoured and blessed. I'd like to say this journey helped me to get there, to find love, but it's a lesson I think I'll be learning for the rest of my life.

Mr X, I don't know who you are but I ask you to be honest with yourself. There is a reason you will not reveal yourself to me and perhaps that reason is one you need to look at the roots of. I wish you well and when you are ready to move on I hope you will allow me to help you on your own journey to love. One day you'll have a dream for your future that will not be based on someone else...it will be all about you.

Thank you for reading, all of you. It has been an honour.

Elise pressed send and closed her email account straight away. She couldn't bear to look at her emails. She didn't know if Taylor would be angry with her or angry at his father for forcing the issue. She was still angry with Nathan and she was angry at Mr X for making her question everything.

Chapter 12

On Friday she slept in until almost midday and awoke to the front doorbell ringing persistently. Eventually she got up to answer it and Nathan was out there. "Why aren't you at work?" She mumbled sleepily, slouching through to the kitchen as he followed her into the house.

"The library called." He sounded unhappy. "There are reporters camped outside. They decided it was best if I didn't go in today."

"Oh." She slumped at the kitchen table and he poured her a coffee. "Are the phones all still unplugged?"

"Yeah." He grinned ruefully. "I didn't plug them in when I left last night. I did keep one on my mobile that I thought would make you laugh." He pulled out his phone and dialled his voicemail, putting it on speakerphone and setting it on the counter between them. There was an automatic voice recording of the time and then the phone crackled.

"Nathan this is your Grandfather. I thought you'd like to know that George Stone has been on the phone asking me to lean on you in the hopes you'd influence that lovely young lady of yours to return to work. I told him he could take his 'lean' and park it between his rear end and something spiky. I assume that was the correct thing to do. Now, I don't know what is going on with the situation but I am deeply upset that you haven't brought her to meet me when your parents are so clearly taken with her. Your mother has agreed to move the family dinner to mine tomorrow. I'll send a car. You did good son. I'm proud of you. She's a corker. Looking forward to seeing you both tomorrow."

He hung up and Elise burst out laughing. "Did he really tell George Stone to sit on something spiky?" She giggled incredulously and Nathan laughed too.

"Yes I think he did."

"Your granddad and I are going to get on brilliantly." Still giggling she finished her coffee and went to get dressed while he made lunch. She hadn't forgiven him, not by a long shot, but he was trying to make it right.

They managed to slip in and out of dance class without being noticed and got back to the flat to find Harry and Amanda sat outside waiting for them.

"We couldn't get either of you on your phones." Harry explained. "We figured you'd be home alone and maybe in need of moral support so we brought dinner and movies and prepaid mobile phones that nobody knows the numbers of."

"If I wasn't so hung up on your brother I think I'd kiss you." Elise joked to Harry as they all entered the flat. "I've been going crazy stuck inside."

"Anyone would." He bumped her shoulder affectionately. "Never mind. Once Grandpa Redwood has met you he'll probably want you to stay out at the mansion with him. Loads of space, top notch security. Much more freedom."

"I wouldn't want to impose." Elise sighed. "I keep thinking I should just go back to Scotland." The other 3 exchanged troubled looks behind her back.

"Don't make any hasty decisions." Nathan told her. "Let it settle for a couple of days. I bet we weren't even on the news today."

Harry visibly winced and Elise stared at him. "What is it?" She demanded. "What was that face for?"

"You haven't seen the news today have you?" He asked miserably. "Haven't you read your blog?"

"No to both." Elise was going pale again. "What's happened?"

"You should read it." He urged.

"I don't want to." Feeling tired and upset, Elise kicked her shoes off. "I'm going for a shower. I'm all sweaty." Without a word she left the room, leaving the others to it.

Nathan helped them empty the bags they'd brought and then went to the computer, switching it on while they crashed on the couches behind him.

"This is really hard on her isn't it?" Amanda asked quietly and Nathan nodded, turning to face her as the computer powered up.

"She's just a regular girl you know? She didn't ask for any of this and it's all just so...alien to her." He ran his hands through his hair leaving it all spiked and messy. "It was just a job and now it's a media circus. The sad thing is that she's so bloody good at what she does. These last few weeks have been a rollercoaster for her but she's genuinely turned these guys' lives around. Her blog is so funny and cute...it's like a little snapshot of her soul and I think people connect with that."

"You really love her don't you?" Harry sounded awed and Nathan nodded, his face lighting up.

"Yeah, I really do." His quirky grin appeared and he spun idly in the chair. "She's amazing. I thank my lucky stars every day that I had the guts to ask her out that day at the library."

"You think she's the one?" Harry grinned. "As in The One with capitals?"

"I *know* she's The One, Harry." He shrugged. "One day, hopefully in the not too distant future, she'll be your sister in law. I just haven't asked her yet. And I know you're going to tell me it's too soon, that it's only been a few weeks, but sometimes you just know. I know and I don't want to lose her."

"I wasn't going to say anything of the sort." Harry protested mildly. "I think she's great and you know I'll welcome her with open arms. I just want you to be happy and I think she makes you happy."

"She does." Nathan turned back to the computer and opened up Elise's blog. "The bastard!" He swore under his breath and Amanda got up and came over.

"What's wrong?" She asked and Nathan sighed.

"Taylor. He edited Elise's blog post. She put that it was going to be her last one and he's removed all reference to it."

"Her last one?" She was surprised. "Elise quit?"

"Yeah she quit." He scrolled down through the comments looking for the one from Mr X that he knew would be there somewhere. "Taylor's father hauled her into his office and when he realised she wasn't going to back down he tried to make her play their media game. She wasn't interested so she quit. Can you believe he called Grandpa and tried to get him to work on us?"

"Really?" Even Harry was astonished at that. "How terribly boys club of him. I hope Papa Redwood told him where to stick it?"

"Of course." Nathan grinned but it soon wilted when he found the response from Mr X. He pointed at the screen. "I take it this is what the news is all about?" He asked and Harry and Amanda both nodded. "Damn it." Nathan looked at his watch and then back at the screen. "Well, we'll tell Elise when she gets out the shower. If she wants to watch it then we will. If not we'll keep ignoring everyone until they get bored and speak to someone else."

When Elise emerged the three of them were sat on the sofa waiting for her looking serious. "You guys look like somebody died." She moved past them into the kitchen and put the kettle on. "Does anyone else want a cuppa?"

"Elise, can you come and sit in here for a minute." Nathan appeared in the kitchen doorway. "We need to talk."

"Okay." Curiously she followed him back to the living room and sat on the sofa opposite. "This feels kinda like an interview." She joked to lighten the mood. "You, me, a table between us..."

Harry cracked smile but Nathan was too worried. "Elise, Mr X is revealing his identity live on television tonight."

"What?" The blood drained out of Elise's head and she swayed dizzily on the sofa.

"He's going as a guest on some talk show." Nathan continued. "It's up to you whether you want to watch but we're more concerned about the media impact. Depending on who it is this could cause a media storm."

"Are you sure you have no idea who it is?" Amanda asked gently.

"It could be anyone." Abruptly she was filled with panic. "We have to get out of the city. What if they find out where I'm staying? Let's book a hotel. Maybe I should fly back to Scotland."

"Calm down." Harry got to his feet and picked up one of the mobiles he had carelessly scattered on the coffee table. "We were supposed to be going to Papa Redwood's tomorrow for dinner. I'll call, tell him we're coming tonight instead. He'll be delighted."

"What about the movies you brought?" Elise asked lamely and Harry shrugged, his grin so like Nathan's.

"We can watch them at Papa's. He won't mind." He raised his phone but Elise was shaking her head.

"No. Don't call him. I need some time to think about this. What time is the tv show?" She jumped to her feet as Harry checked his watch.

"It's in about an hour."

"Give me some time." Rushing through to the study she closed the door behind her and powered up the computer. He had to have emailed her. There's no way he would go live on TV without some sort of private warning.

Her inbox was flooded with hundreds of messages and she scrolled through them frantically, trying to find the ones from today. She missed it the first time and then, on the second read through, her heart stopped.

To: Elise Waterford <internal>
CC: Mr X (X_Towers@hotmail.com)
From: Taylor Stone <internal>

SUBJECT: It's me. I'm Mr X.

Elise,
This is going to come as something of a shock and I'm sorry for that. I've tried to call but can't get through and, when I came round to explain, you weren't in. My father told me that he'd fucked up and you'd resigned. I thought my heart was going to shatter when I got your latest blog post and you said it was your last.

Please Elise, I beg you. Don't go back to Scotland. You wanted me to be honest so I'm being honest. I'm going on television tonight to tell everyone it was me. I'm going to own up to everything so there can be no doubt how I feel about you. I don't care what my family thinks and this media circus has gone on for long enough. It's time to put a stop to it.

I think I've loved you since the moment I laid eyes on you. You were just so damn funny swearing like a trooper, all flustered. I knew for definite you'd captured my heart when you put me in my place that night at the chalet. I know I've been an idiot, Elise. I know I don't deserve a second chance. I just wanted to prove to you that I wasn't the shallow playboy you thought I was, that I genuinely cared and you weren't just some tumble to me. All these weeks it's hurt to hear so many people casually saying I couldn't be Mr X because I didn't have a romantic bone in my body. I do. I tried to show it in the only way I knew how without screwing up my career and yours. I know how painful it is to be tarred with nepotism. I messed up and it snowballed totally out of control.

I should have just come to you directly when you arrived in London, but I thought you were angry with me because you hadn't returned any of my communications. By the time I found out it was Anton, it was too late. I've spent *so many hours this last week wondering what would have happened if he hadn't interfered, if we had kept in touch, if you could have maybe come to love me in those months, if Nathan wouldn't have been in the picture because I was there already, if I had kissed you at the ball when I wanted to so very much...*

You were so honest with me when you emailed, when I was just Mr X and not Taylor Stone. I guess I forgot sometimes that you didn't know who I was. I could hear your voice reading the words even as my eyes picked them from the screen. I meant every word I said to you.

I'm sorry. More sorry than you'll ever know. I really do love you and I hope that you'll forgive me one day because it's too much to hope now that you would love me in return.
Ever yours,
Taylor xxx

Elise sat there, her mind reeling as she read it again. This was so many colours of fucked up she could paint a whole damn rainbow with it.

"You were emailing Mr X?" Nate demanded. "Why didn't you say anything?" She'd been so absorbed reading the email she hadn't heard him come in behind her and she realised he'd read the whole thing over her shoulder.

"Because I knew you'd fly off the handle with jealousy," she replied honestly.

"And you think that makes it okay to speak to your secret admirer behind my back?" His voice was incredulous and she couldn't blame him.

"No. It doesn't. It's not okay, but I couldn't help myself. I was so curious about who he was and then he turned out to be funny and intelligent. It seemed rude not to reply to his emails." Filled with shame, she hung her head.

"I can't fucking deal with this." He stormed out the room and she suddenly felt herself flooded with anger. He couldn't deal with it?

"You can't fucking deal with this?" she yelled, following him out into the living room. "You think it's okay to not tell me who you are, but I have to tell you everything that happens every goddamn minute of my life? I'm not allowed to have a private conversation with anyone?" Harry and Amanda gaped at them from the sofa as they shouted at each other.

"This guy is leaving you love letters and all this time you've been lying to me, swearing blind that you don't care, that you're not curious about him. You lied to me!"

"And you lied to me!" she yelled back. "Do you have any idea how it feels to wake up and find out from the news that the guy you thought was a nice, quiet librarian is actually a bazillionaire? Do you have any idea how stupid that made me feel?"

"But it's okay for your precious Taylor to lie to you all this time, just because he said he was rich up front?"

She gasped at the nastiness of it. "First off, he's not 'my' anything. Secondly, he's never actually lied to me. I never asked Taylor if he was Mr X because I just assumed he wasn't. And for the record, in all my emails with Mr X he's been honest about everything except his name. It's a long time since I've had a conversation that honest with anyone."

"Well aren't you two just the happy couple?" Nathan sneered. "Do you love him?"

"What the hell sort of a question is that?" Elise gaped.

"A pretty fucking simple one. Do you love him?"

"We've been together all these weeks and you still have to ask me that?" Elise abruptly burst into tears. "I can't do this anymore. I'm going home to Scotland." She grabbed her handbag and Harry finally jumped into motion.

"You can't, not at this time of night, Elise." He took her bag from her and pulled her into a hug, moving her away from where Nathan was visibly shaking with rage. "I think you've both fucked up quite considerably in this relationship, but right now, with everything that's going on, it's not the time to make rash decisions. I'm going to take Nate home and Amanda is going to stay here with you. We can all have a calm discussion about this in the morning when some of the steam has blown off, okay?"

"Okay." She snuffled and he handed her over to Amanda, almost forcibly bundling Nathan out of the flat.

"Try and get some sleep." He called back over his shoulder and then they were gone, leaving Elise shaking in Amanda's arms.

Easy words to say, but Elise wasn't really surprised when she found herself in the kitchen at 6am having barely slept a wink. She hadn't watched the TV show and her phone was still switched off. She hadn't even looked at her emails. She'd been lying awake wondering how she had ever found herself in this crazy situation and the more she thought about it, the more she realised that it just wasn't her. All she'd ever wanted was to settle down somewhere quiet, maybe get married and have a child or two. She just wanted to write books. This was too much.

As the thought settled in, she became more and more homesick for her little cottage in the highlands and that finally decided it for her. Plugging in the house phone, she called directory enquiries and asked to be put through to the airline that had flown her down. There was a flight leaving for Inverness just after half nine, so she booked a seat on it. She was going home. Once her payment had gone through for them, she looked up the number for a taxi company in the house folder and called them too. They agreed to send one for her as soon as possible, so she threw a few things in a bag, grabbed her guitar, scribbled a note for Amanda and then crept out of the flat to wait. By the time 7am had come around, she was on her way to the airport.

The taxi driver gave her a curious look as she handed him the money and then he cleared his throat. "Do I know you from somewhere?" He asked and she winced.

"Only if you've been watching the news for the last week. I'm the woman that's about to break the hearts of two really nice, good and kind men." Feeling like a grade A bitch, she grabbed her guitar case and got out of the car, hurrying into the terminal building. It seemed like there were newspapers everywhere with pictures of Taylor and a few of her on the front page, but she tried to ignore them as she checked in. The woman behind the check-in desk opened her passport and did a double-take, glancing at her speculatively as she processed the boarding pass and handed her documents back.

"Are you sure about this?" she asked suddenly. "I know it's not my place but that Taylor Stone is a bit of a dish."

"He is, but I don't belong in his world." Elise pocketed her ticket. "Happily ever after is for fairytales. I'm no Cinderella."

"Well that's a shame. But best of luck." The check-in assistant smiled brightly at her and Elise nodded, too weary to reply. As she walked away, she realised that this was what being a celebrity must feel like, everyone having an opinion on your life whether you invited it or not. The thought was depressing.

She put her hand luggage through security and killed the time waiting for her flight to board absently browsing the duty free. She'd left in such a rush that she hadn't had an opportunity to buy anything for Fern. Spotting her friend's favourite perfume, she bought her a large bottle and left it at that. It wasn't particularly anything to do with London, but Elise didn't even want to think about the city she was leaving right now. Such a wasted opportunity...and all because of two men. All those museums she should have visited, the shows she should have seen...it *was* a waste. Perhaps when this didn't all hurt so much, she'd come back and visit her projects. Perhaps she could come back for a wedding, if they were successful. The thought made her smile.

Finally it was time to board and, as the plane took off, she leaned back in her seat and closed her eyes, glad it was all behind her.

By the time she got back to her village, she'd decided to go straight to Fern's. She'd be frantic by now, not knowing what the hell was going on and with Elise's phone still switched off. When Fern opened the door, she gaped at Elise for a moment and then dragged her into a stiff bear hug. Before she knew what was happening Elise had burst into tears and just sobbed and sobbed until she felt like she was going to drown the whole world.

"You poor thing." Fern pulled her into the kitchen, parked her at the table with a roll of kitchen towel and then set about making her some tea. "Have you even eaten today? You look exhausted. I'll make some tea and here's a slice of cake. You'll stay for lunch. And maybe dinner. I've got a movie we can watch this afternoon to take your mind off things. What happened? You should have let me know you were coming."

"I didn't know until this morning and I couldn't face switching my phone on to call you." Elise tried to dry her eyes but they just kept welling up again. "I'm sorry, I know this is pathetic. I just can't seem to stop."

"It's not pathetic at all. What made you come back? I thought you and Nate were going to try and ride it out."

"We were. Until he discovered I'd been emailing Mr X trying to find out who he was. He went nuts and started shouting at me because I hadn't told him. It got pretty nasty."

Fern winced. "Did you watch the program? You do know who Mr X is now, right?"

"I didn't watch it, but I didn't need to. He sent me an email to tell me he was going to do it. I was reading it last night when Nate came in. That's what sparked the argument."

"I'm glad it was Taylor," Fern said after a moment. "I think secretly I was always rooting for him. I can't work out if you're crying over him or Nate." Elise shrugged.

"The whole thing is a total mess. I just wanted to come home. I know it was probably the cowardly thing to do, but I couldn't breathe in the city. It was starting to feel like a prison. I'm just not emotionally ready to face Taylor yet, and as for Nate...when you start a relationship with so much lying between you, I don't know how you come back from that. To love each other, you have to be able to trust each other and I think that's lost forever. It's got echoes of Max all over again."

"Well I'm glad you're home." Fern set a cup of tea down in front of Elise and gave her another quick hug around the shoulders. "I missed you while you were gone. Come on, drink your tea and then we'll go watch films and laugh until we forget you've even been away."

Chapter 13

Two days later, Elise went into the local courier and begged for her old job back. Pleased to have something of a celebrity working for them, they didn't make her try too hard and over the next couple of weeks she settled back into life in her cottage. It seemed so quiet compared to the hustle and bustle of the city, but Elise knew she'd never take it for granted again.

After ten days she'd finally been brave enough to turn her phone on but was screening calls and slowly they tailed off. Nathan hadn't even tried to contact her and she realised she'd probably really hurt him with her disappearing act on top of the argument. She felt full of shame for not even having left him a note, but reasoned that it took two to fight for a relationship and he had yelled some pretty nasty things during the row. Her email inbox had remained unopened. She wasn't ready to face whatever was there from Taylor.

She had steadfastly stayed away from reading the newspapers or watching the news on television, so she was a little surprised when Fern let herself into Elise's house unannounced one morning and slapped a newspaper on her desk.

"You need to read this." She said decisively and then walked out. Elise gaped after her for a moment and then looked at the paper. Taylor was on the front page with the headline "Heartbroken Editor Lays It All on the Line!" For a long moment she was tempted to just tear it up, but she knew Fern wouldn't have brought it if she didn't think it was important. Setting it on the table she made a cup of tea, fetched a box of tissues and then began to read.

Following rumours of a split between Elise Waterford and Nathan Redwood, fuelled by the former's shock decision to return to her home in the Scottish Highlands, we can now report that Taylor Stone, millionaire playboy editor of Monochrome Magazine, the highest grossing magazine in Europe, has decided not to give up on her without a fight. Sources close to the six-time winner of the Most Eligible Bachelor UK award say he has resigned from his post at Monochrome and followed Ms Waterford to Scotland, where he is staying at his holiday home in Aviemore while he tries to decide how to win her back. Friends and relatives have been speculating about their relationship since Taylor Stone put all of his London properties on the market ten days ago, only four days after confessing his love for Ms Waterford live on national television. There are also rumours that he purchased a set of prints from a photography session with Ms Waterford at a well-known gallery. There has been no response to his unmasking as the mysterious Mr X from Ms Waterford but we are led to believe that she knows Mr X is Mr Stone. She was unavailable for comment at the time of printing. A spokesperson for Mr Stone confirmed that the thirty-three year old had indeed resigned from the magazine and was asking for people to respect his privacy while he retreated to Scotland to think about his future. A source at Monochrome was heard saying she hopes Taylor and Elise get together. "They're both such sweet people and he is clearly head over heels in love with her." It seems in these times of financial hardship and depression that everyone would like, for once, to see a Cinderella story with a happy ending.

Epilogue

To: Mr X (_X_Towers@hotmail.com_)
From: Elise Waterford (_CinderellaoftheHighlands_
@hotmail.com)

X,

I'm writing because I need your advice. I trusted you
with my biggest secret so I guess I can trust you with my
heart. You see, there's this guy. I really like him. He's smart,
funny, gorgeous in a very rugged and GQ way. He's
romantic and sweet and writes the cutest little love letters.
The thing is, I totally fucked up. He told me he loved me and
instead of dealing with it in an appropriate and adult
manner, I totally freaked out and ran away. I don't know if
he'll forgive me, even when I tell him how sorry I am and
confess to being a total idiot. And even if he does forgive
me, I still don't know that we should be together. When
we're alone away from the city and it's just the two of us,
we get on like a house on fire, but his family totally
disapprove of me and I don't want to drive a wedge
between them. He's worked so damn hard to get where he
is and I couldn't live with myself if I messed it up for him. I'm
also hurting from the nasty break-up of a recent
relationship. This guy I like? He's too good to be a rebound
guy. I'm so torn...part of me wants to turn up at his house in
Aviemore and sing him Ronan Keating wearing nothing but
my guitar to prove to him that I really want to try and I'm
sorry, but part of me wants to just keep my head down and
hope that one day my heart stops hurting. What should I
do?

Elise

To: Elise Waterford
(_CinderellaoftheHighlands@hotmail.com_)

From: Mr X (X_Towers@hotmail.com)

Elise,
The guitar option. Definitely. NOW.
Ever yours,
X

P.S. If he let you leave the first time round he sounds like a bit of a tool but, you know, if you love him I'm sure you can overlook that, right?

P.P.S. LOVING the new email address Cinders!

P.P.P.S. Please don't drive naked. You'll get arrested. You can undress when you get there. Just try not to break anything.

P.P.P.P.S. Love you x

***

To: Elise Waterford
(CinderellaoftheHighlands@hotmail.com)
From: Mr X (X_Towers@hotmail.com)

Cinders,
You look spectacularly beautiful today. That dress is really something. Special occasion?
Ever yours,
X

To: Mr X (X_Towers@hotmail.com)
From: Elise Waterford (CinderellaoftheHighlands @hotmail.com)

X,

I got married this afternoon to some dude I used to work for. You might have seen him. He's looking rather sexy in his suit. I'm not sure if I can bear to wait until later to let him see what's underneath the dress...
Cinders xxx

To: Elise Waterford (CinderellaoftheHighlands@hotmail.com)
From: Mr X (X_Towers@hotmail.com)

Cinders,
I don't think he's sure he can wait either (o_o) In fact, I suspect if you met him in your hotel room in about four minutes time, you'd be able to confirm that speculation first hand.
Ever yours,
X

***

To: Mr X (X_Towers@hotmail.com)
From: Elise Waterford (CinderellaoftheHighlands @hotmail.com)

X,
I 'm thinking of getting a tattoo. Any ideas on what my husband would find acceptable? I'd hate to get something that would irritate him.
Cinders xxx

To: Elise Waterford (CinderellaoftheHighlands@hotmail.com)
From: Mr X (X_Towers@hotmail.com)

Cinders,
A tattoo? Really? Well, if you're certain, then I recommend you get a cupcake. A little one with a snowflake

on. And then around the edges you can have the words "I don't come in batches of 12".
Ever yours,
X

***

To: Mr X (X_Towers@hotmail.com**)**
From: Elise Waterford (CinderellaoftheHighlands@hotmail.com**)**

X,
Need your advice again. You know my husband and I have been trying for kids for a while now? What do you think is the best way to tell him I'm pregnant?
Cinders xxx

To: Elise Waterford (CinderellaoftheHighlands@hotmail.com**)**
From: Mr X (X_Towers@hotmail.com**)**

Cinders,
I vote for the naked guitar playing. It went down so well the first time.
Ever yours,
X

To: Elise Waterford (CinderellaoftheHighlands@hotmail.com**)**
From: Mr X (X_Towers@hotmail.com**)**

*WAIT WHAT?!?!?! PREGNANT!!!! *faints**

***

To: Mr X (X_Towers@hotmail.com**)**

From: Elise Waterford (CinderellaoftheHighlands @hotmail.com)

X,
Any idea where I'd get a fairy godmother costume? I've been invited to Project 1's wedding and they specified they thought it would be the most appropriate outfit for me. Apparently Mark has bought me the wand he promised all those months ago. They are clearly nuts but I said I'd do it. Wings and all. I'd invite you as my plus one, but my husband already thinks it's weird that I'm having an extra-marital affair with his alter ego.
Cinders xxx

To: Elise Waterford (CinderellaoftheHighlands@hotmail.com)
From: Mr X (X_Towers@hotmail.com)

Cinders,
Weird is one word. I prefer kinky.
Ever yours,
X

To: Mr X (X_Towers@hotmail.com)
From: Elise Waterford (CinderellaoftheHighlands @hotmail.com)

X,
You're the editor. I bow to your superior linguistic prowess.
Cinders xxx

To: Elise Waterford (CinderellaoftheHighlands@hotmail.com)
From: Mr X (X_Towers@hotmail.com)

Cinders,

I just...wow...there are too many openings in that to even start with. I love you, you know that right?
Ever yours,
X

To: Mr X (<u>X_Towers@hotmail.com</u>**)**
From: Elise Waterford (<u>CinderellaoftheHighlands</u>
<u>@hotmail.com</u>**)**

X,
Every day of always my love.
Cinders xxx

If you have enjoyed this, please leave me a review on Amazon or Goodreads, and tell your friends about my books. As an independent author, I rely on word of mouth!

Rivka Spicer has been writing since she was twelve years old. Now in her thirties, she is the author of twenty-two novels and seven novellas, with further publications planned in 2023. With a background in science and a career in criminal justice behind her, she is now living in France with her partner, indulging in her many hobbies and enjoying the food.

Writing as Rivka Spicer:

Masquerade Series
Masquerade
Carnevale
Obsession

The Last Ancient Trilogy
Sage
Marked
Coven

Four Seasons/Sisters Dark Series
Summer Loving
Winter's Edge (coming soon)

Stand-alone novels
The Broken Souls
Enclave
A Kiss from the Grave
Saltire Rising

Novellas
Beautiful of Heart

Writing as Ivory Quinn:

Darkness Falls Series
Obsession: Darkness Falls
Redemption: Darkness Falls

Blue: Darkness Falls
Jax: Darkness Falls

Stand-alone novels
The Seven Veils

Novellas:
The Sessions: Elienne
The Sessions: James
The Sessions: Jax
The Sessions: Lana
The Night Palace

Writing as Aurora Maris:

The Fractals Series:
Marked by Monsters
Committed to Monsters
Captured by Ghosts
Cherished by Ghosts
Seduced by Monsters
Novellas:
The Demonae's Cabin

Made in the USA
Las Vegas, NV
04 February 2025

17518554R00118